Meera Rising

A Short Story

Nandita Chakraborty

First published by Busybird Publishing 2017

ISBN
Print: 978-1-925585-69-8
Ebook: 978-1-925585-70-4

Cover image: Kev Howltt
Cover: Blaise van Hecke
Author Photo: Rebecca Olsen
Cover design: Busybird Publishing
Layout and typesetting: Busybird Publishing
Editor: Beau Hillier

Busybird Publishing
2/118 Para Road
Montmorency, Victoria
Australia 3094
www.busybird.com.au

Inspired by the life of Meera

For Benjamin

Prologue

Brian rubbed the dust out of his eyes to see who his Good Samaritan was. He looked in awe. It felt hard to breathe, as if he were in a trance – some sort of a mystical dream, or an out of body experience.

She smiled at him; Brian remembered that same smile from when he first met her.

The only thing he could say was, 'Mcera!'

The Arrival

'Ladies and gentlemen, welcome to Indira Gandhi International Airport. Please remain seated until the seat belt sign is switched off. The outside temperature is thirteen degrees Celsius. We hope you had a pleasant flight and we look forward to flying with you again.'

Meera looked outside the plane window as it touched down on the land that she once called home. She could see the cold mist blanketing the terminal outside and felt somewhat helpless. She wanted to vanish with the mist.

No turning back now, Meera – this is it, she whispered to herself.

'Excuse me, did you say something to me?'

Aware of being watched by her fellow passenger, she quickly regained her composure and shook her head to apologise.

Outside, her parents would be waiting to receive her, a decade-old tradition of receiving and saying goodbye at the airport. With time, everything has taken a subtle turn: no more screams of enthusiastic aunties, uncles, first cousins and second cousins waiting along with Mum and Dad at the arrival gate. The same can be said for the departure gate: no more teary screams from anxious relatives. But Meera knew there would be no departures from here on.

Walking towards the baggage area, she looked around; how much things have changed, now with no difference between two countries. It sounded very cliché to her, but she felt east had definitely met west now. The new airport was a testament to this. The modern airport and the largest democracy of the world were showing off their richest attributes. If only the people of the largest democracy could now change the way they thought. *Is marriage the only solution to complete a woman? Is it always necessary for a man to be a plan?* Meera thought.

It had taken four years for her to sum up the courage to finally say yes to settling down. Would it take another few decades to finally say she wants to be in love? Maybe she was in love. She didn't have any answers. Maybe this was the final sacrifice, or a compromise. Maybe it was the final answer to love. With all these conflicting thoughts, Meera collected her baggage and made her way to the arrival gate.

She saw her parents waiting for her, her legs heavy with anxiety; she had the sinking feeling of her freedom of expression being lost forever. Meera touched her parents' feet to seek their blessings – that made Mr and Mrs Sen beam with happiness. They were proud of their daughter, that even though she'd stayed in another part of the world for the past ten years she hadn't forgotten the deep sense of her culture and tradition. 'Welcome home!' Mr Sen said softly while hugging his thirty-three year old daughter.

The trip to the house was somewhat mellow; no one spoke much, apart from on the weather overseas and how cold it was here. Mr and Mrs Sen tried their best to cheer their daughter and hide the helplessness they felt for her; on the other hand, Meera tried her best to tap into their positivism and hide her despair.

The traffic, the horns, the people, the new fly-overs – and all around was so much greenery. She lowered her car window just a little bit to engage with the moving world outside. The damp air was thick with the sweet smell of rain and smog hazed the vision of the motorists. She felt calm, as if the fog was a quilt protecting her from her fears. The fumes from the scooters intoxicating the air was not that much of a bother to her. The scooter riders had helmets on their heads; to her that was a revelation, people minding rules.

The car suddenly stopped – a traffic jam.

'Ten rupees a garland to wash your sin, ten rupees a garland …' A little boy with a basket full of rose and jasmine garlands leapt out of nowhere, as if he was always there to take advantage of the traffic chaos on a cold night. This little genius salesman was knocking on every car window, trying to haggle down the alluring garlands in the name of God. 'Just ten rupees, Aunty. Oh! Uncle, buy for Aunty, your wife and God will bless you forever for eternity!' He changed his lines according to the occupants of the car. Meera laughed at it, and so did Mr and Mrs Sen.

The sweet intoxicating smell of the jasmine combined with the incense coming from a makeshift temple around the corner, where people were queued to offer their prayers. Meera lowered her head and folded her hands in a soft prayer. The excitement of seeing people everywhere never bothered her, as now she was among her kind. Once, she used to offer prayers like this while Mr Sen drove her to school. It was all coming back into her life.

Her thoughts were suddenly interrupted by a loud voice. 'Oh! *Bhai dekh ke*! (Brother watch it!)' screamed a tuk-tuk (auto-rickshaw) driver weaving its way through the halted traffic. He was blaring out some modern music, providing a few seconds of entertainment to the disgruntled traffickers. She assumed herself to be one of them.

Once again on the road, she was amazed to see the old frail-looking bus had taken the shape of the Ventura buses by the Yarra. To Meera, everything was the same yet so different. She thought her mind was playing tricks on her.

The car halted yet again in one of the traffic lights. 'Sorry, dear, these are the last lights before home.' Mr Sen winked at his daughter.

She turned her head to see her old college from Mrs Sen's window. The walls of the college were covered by political posters; the symbol of lotus and hand dominated it with the words, 'Vote for us.' Meera smirked; whoever posted them made sure people who passed by also read the sign, 'Posting posters here is strictly prohibited.' Next to the college was the same chai stall that sold tea to the hundreds of college students, some late for their lectures and some bunking their lectures. It was still there, only now as a refurbished establishment. 'Remarkable,' Meera whispered. 'Wait! Stop the car, Dad.'

Mr Sen was surprised by his daughter's odd request. He asked what the matter was.

'Dad, could you please pull over on the side? I have to

visit someone there.' Pointing at the tea stall, Meera finally broke into a smile.

'Come now, let's go home dear, you can have chai at home.' Mrs Sen tried to stop Meera but she was too careless to hear anything. As soon as the car came to a halt she jumped from her seat and ran towards the tea stall.

'Let her go! Let her cherish her past. Come, Mrs Sen, let's have some tea.' Mr Sen touched his wife's hand to stop her from holding Meera back from her adventure.

As Meera entered the tea stall, the smell of ginger and cinnamon mixed with the aroma of freshly cooked bread churned up her stomach. She hadn't eaten for almost six hours, but that was soon forgotten when she was welcomed with a huge smile by the owner, who had now taken his place on the white tiled wall. The photo had a garland, and the smell of the incense stick next to the photo gave Meera a brief idea of his demise. A small boy came running towards them to take their order.

'Masala dosa, vada, omelette, chow mein or chai. Don't ask for coffee because we don't serve it here. If you want to have coffee go to the Costa café next door, this is "Desi style" roadside chai stall.'

Meera burst out in laughter at the enthusiast waiter, who she assumed must be at least twelve or thirteen years old. 'Okay! Okay! We will have all that you make in your "local" style chai stall, but first tell me how old you are.'

'Fourteen. That's my father in the photo, who recently passed away, and the one you see in the corner making tea is my older brother. You could say I am the owner too.'

She smiled and felt guilty for not coming here any sooner. She'd lovingly called the previous owner Chai Chacha. The death of her 'tea uncle' somewhat closed the doors of the past, inviting Meera to look forward to the future – which made her uncomfortable.

'I used to study in the college next to your chai stall. It was made of just brick but today to see your stall in concrete and white tiles, I am very happy. Three teas and all that you have just recited.'

'Yes! *Didi* (sister) all coming up, my name is Raju.' Raju flashed his whole set of teeth to the newly acquainted diners and ran into the kitchen.

Mr and Mrs Sen were far too obligated to their daughter. They had to go with her choice of dining, in the middle of the cold winter night. At least they were happy to see her smiling and making conversations with her newly acquainted friend, who called Meera his older sister.

The bungalow where Meera's parents resided was in one of the posh neighbourhoods in the south of the city. The Maruti Suzuki 800s and the trusted Ambassador cars were now all but replaced with the likes of the west; the odd Lamborghinis and the persistent Audis stood outside the equally immaculate bungalows, mocking the scarce Ambassador taxis that passed their ways. She could hear the occasional beeping of the horns from the main road and the sounds and laughs from the kitchens of the neighbouring bungalows. Some of the watchman guarding these houses sat inside their booths listening to their radios. There was a laundryman delivering clothes and pedestrians walking their dogs. *Some things will never change*, Meera thought to herself.

The watchman opened the gates for Mr Sen to park his car inside the driveway of his bungalow. The smell of the freshly painted bungalow was churning up the chai and chow mein in Meera's belly. Jetlag was slowly slipping into her.

Mr Sen called, 'Ramu, Ramu, where are you?'

'Coming!' A frail-looking, thin man in his late twenties

with hair parted in the middle of his head, his white pyjamas standing out in the dark, came running from the annexe of the bungalow.

'I told you to light up the house, why didn't you?' said Mr Sen.

'But, *Sahib*, you said you would call me when you were five minutes away from the house.'

Mr Sen was slightly annoyed with the help's direct remark. 'Okay! Okay! Now will you be standing here all night? Go and light up the house, and if it's not much of a bother come back to help us with the luggage.' The startled boy ran quickly before his boss could have another outburst. 'These servants nowadays are good for nothing – hope his wife is more cluey and dependable.'

'I haven't seen him before,' said Meera.

Meera turned to Mrs Sen while adjusting her bag on her shoulder. 'New! He is new in the city too, he was sent to us by the local servants' centre where we had written an application for help.'

'Servants' centre? Wow, things have surely changed here.' A huge reflection of the bungalow suddenly glinted on the car; the entire place lit up like a Christmas tree. Meera turned back and saw the colossal bungalow dipped in strings of intricate lights. The fresh white paint only made it look royal, fit to be a king's palace.

'Good job, Ramu! Good job! This boy has talent!' Mr Sen screamed at the top of his voice.

Ramu came running from inside to see his masterpiece. He looked at Meera and smiled to himself. 'Congratulations in advance for your engagement.'

Both Mr and Mrs Sen hugged an overwhelmed Meera. She didn't know how to react, but she did know Thursday was her engagement and next Sunday was her wedding.

The Sens

Meera Sen never had despairs in her life, nor did she have regrets. However, she did contemplate what life would have been if it didn't turn out the way it had. Being the only child in the family, there was no fierce competition to compete with siblings – her only competition was herself. To excel better in her studies was no pressure; the only pressure was to please her ego. Perfectionist was not a right word for her – realist, yes.

Mr Sen always wanted a son, but when he saw Meera for the first time in the nursery cot, all his longing for a son was put to rest when her little hand closed around his finger. A teardrop touched his face and he was proud to be her father.

On the other hand, Mrs Sen never complained – her secret wish was always to have a daughter.

During school, Meera's only wish was to be a doctor. She would often be the only one sitting in her classroom during lunch breaks, either hidden behind a book of science or already solving equations of her maths homework. She had few friends in school, always being bullied for her glasses and for the coconut oil in her hair. It was always massaged in her hair and later neatly done up in plaits. 'Look, the coconut oil factory has entered the classroom, let's bow down to Miss Coconut of class nine.' The boys would often tease her and slowly she would walk to her desk with her head held down.

She was often seen kneeling outside the principal's office. Once her parents were called and were advised to take her out of school.

Meera's only friend in school was Lalita; it seemed that Lalita's only concern in life was to watch out for Meera and bully those who would bully her. Her being friends with Meera was by accident. Lalita was weak in maths and would often fail in the subject; she was asked by the teachers to stay after class to take extra coaching. Being alone in a classroom with the maths teacher drove Lalita mad. She asked Meera for help so she could spend some time mastering the art of equations, and on the other hand, Meera asked Lalita to mentor her in the self-esteem she lacked. Both had a strange bond. During exam times, Lalita would spend hours learning maths with Meera.

It was quite convenient for the girls, as they both lived in the same area. Mr and Mrs Sen were both very happy to see their daughter thrive in school. They often asked Meera to invite Lalita home, but Meera would always conspire against this. 'She is busy, Maa; I don't think it will be a good idea.'

Years and years of travelling – cities after cities, making new friends while losing some old ones – had made it difficult for the Sens. The nature of Mr Sen's business made it difficult for Meera to make friends and be social. Meera felt closer to her solitude then the company of others – hence, she created her own world of biology and maths as her best friends. She was very particular about her possessions though. To be precise, she knew exactly who borrowed her *Nancy Drew* and to whom she had lent her favourite colour pencils.

It was only during this time when Mr and Mrs Sen decided they had to be fair to their only child. To see their daughter making friends for the first time was priceless; such was Mr Sen's love for Meera that he bought the house in one of the rich localities of the state and made it his office too.

When Meera finished college, it was decided by her father that she should be sent overseas to finish her masters in microbiology. She was not happy with the decision but she thought her father had the best interest for her, so she quietly obeyed.

'Lalita, I am scared … I don't know how I will be able to cope there.' Meera, almost in tears, lowered her eyes.

'Don't worry, I will be there with you.' Comforting words from Lalita brought back a smile on Meera's face.

***

The clothes from the cupboards were all over the place. Shoes on the bed and socks on the floor did not make any sense to Mrs Sen. She wanted to scream at her daughter's ignorance but she let it go today. At the back of her mind she was thinking of how she brought up Meera, protecting her, making her co-dependent, wrapping her in cotton wool with no room for thorns to grow during her upbringing. Mrs Sen always gave her daughter what she'd been deprived of. With that thought, today she shadowed her eyes with the same cotton wool she'd used for nurturing baby Meera. She was nervous of her little baby leaving the nest; somehow she knew it will be the best for her.

'My darling, look, Ravi *mama* is here to see you.'

Meera sprung from her bed to see her favourite uncle, her mother's only brother.

'Well, well! Look who is going to make all the difference in the Sen family.' Ravi Dasgupta was a priest, always cynical of the Sens' plot of being adventurous. He was totally against the idea of Meera leaving for overseas. The idea of her being modern was tearing him up inside. To him, 'modern' was snipping the long skirt to a mini skirt and showing skin. To him, a good Hindu shouldn't indulge in glasses of wine and endless parties that had no meaning for the soul.

Meera had no clue of her uncle's ideas of being a good priest. She just adored him for reading her stories about Lord Krishna when she was five. According to Meera, no one could be more dramatic and animated than him. The stories of Krishna would miss all the theatrics if told by anyone other than Ravi *mama*. He would take her to a magical place where she would visualise Lord Krishna and Radha as two fantasy characters like Peter Pan and Cinderella. When she grew up, she replaced them with the likes of *The Lord of the Rings* and *Harry Potter*, but slowly she began to fantasise the love of Krishna for Radha in all the movie romances. She often thought of them as a commoner's answer to an extraordinary reality.

'Meera, come here my beauty, I have something for

you.' Ravi Dasgupta took out an idol of Lord Krishna from his cloth bag. While handing it to Meera, he looked at her and with a huge smile he said, 'Let there be the love of Lord Krishna always with you – always.'

Mrs Sen did not want Mr Sen to see her brother's little gift to Meera. In fact, it was the same gift that Ravi Dasgupta wanted to give Meera on her fifth birthday. Mr Sen was quite angry with the choice of the gift – not that he didn't have faith. It was just that he was against feeding religion into a child from a tender age of five. There were arguments and in one instance he insulted Ravi Dasgupta. 'Religion is for those who have no hope. My daughter has me.'

Those words kept ringing in Mrs Sen's ears. 'Come on, Meera; pack it away in your suitcase before your dad comes in the room.'

Ravi Dasgupta didn't want any insults today – not because he was scared of Mr Sen, but because he wanted his only niece to go with a happy heart. Like an obedient child, he approved of Mrs Sen's remarks and helped Meera pack away the idol of Krishna.

Lives by the River Yarra

Looking outside the window, Meera watched the tiny droplets of rain that created ripples on the Yarra River. She thought about the sign she read next to a pond a few days ago: 'Water wears all colours and owns none'. She felt like that today. Six years in this land; she had been so scared to call it her home. Now the doubt and fear had blossomed into trust and appreciation of the city had grown deep within her.

Today it was different. She was not only homesick but had the urgency of belonging somewhere, to someone.

She felt lost, hopeless and sad. She looked at the idol of Krishna. Closing her eyes to a silent prayer, she whispered, 'I need a reason to be here … or a reason not to be here. Can't you see I have a feeling of helplessness?' For a long time Meera looked at the idol of Krishna – then, taking her umbrella, she slowly made her way to the door to begin her day.

***

The laboratory was in the university campus where she was working. It was four tram stops away. She could have easily walked but the sombre mood and the weather made her stop for the tram.

Carefully excusing herself from the morning crowd, she took refuge next to a group of men. Laughing and swearing loudly were some of the attributes of men that annoyed Meera. One of them was smoking so heavily next to her that she had to tell him off. 'Do you mind?'

'Sorry!' the stubbly-faced man replied very politely to Meera.

She was still not impressed. 'You shouldn't be smoking in a tram stop, it's unlawful,' Meera said with contempt in her voice.

He thought she was not only rude but a grumpy young woman. 'You okay, Brian?' One of the men from the group asked the stubbled man, looking at him with a frown.

'It's okay, Dan, an FOB I guess. This one is a brick short of the cart load,' Brian said to his mate Dan, pointing his index finger to his head. He made sure Meera heard it too, thinking she would now back off.

Meera didn't budge; instead, she made a choice to stick up for herself. It was open war. 'Hey! Mate, I am bright enough to know that I am not "fresh off the boat" and I am definitely not a grumpy middle aged man smoking his lungs away and forcing others to do the same too. Get a life, dude. I think I can provide you that brick which is short off your head.'

Meera stormed into the tram, leaving Brian speechless. His green eyes were shining and his lips broke into a smile. He laughed, winking at her. Others laughed with Brian, some clapped.

Brian's Story

Brian Johnson was a country bumpkin born to a chicken farmer. He hated his country lifestyle; with any given opportunity he would be seen in the local pub. He had the build of a rugged country man with an average five foot eleven inches height. He not only had the devil's charm to match his humour, but also a mesmerising smile that complemented his green eyes and his sandy brown hair. The dimples on his chin were a prominent feature that could make any woman go weak on her knees. His good looks made him ordinary, not because there were countless men in both the city and the country just like him (or better looking than him) but because he was a sly, cunning chicken farmer who cashed in on his good looks and intelligence. He was indeed a ladies' man.

He would often be seen arguing – if not with the local butcher, haggling him for money, then with the owner of the local milk bar – or making small talk with local hoons. In the country fair he would often be seen with his father selling chickens and eggs, and during any given break, he would run to the Ferris wheel for a ride with the local kids. Whatever anyone said about Brian, he had a softer part to his personality.

On his thirtieth birthday, he was given a camera; he became so engrossed in this new toy that he would explore the whole town and capture its mesmerising beauty on his lens. His work was published in the local newspaper and that caught the eye of a reputable newspaper in the city. Brian joined as an intern and drifted into foreign correspondence; he got his first big break when he was covering a story in Afghanistan with a well-known journalist. His photos made headlines around the world; he captured the struggle of life so beautifully in his camera that he earned a Walkley Award.

It was nearly fifteen years since that story; now forty-four, Brian had established himself as a well-known photographer and face in journalism. Winning many accolades for his work still did not change the country bumpkin in him. At any given chance, he would escape to the country to recharge away from the chaos of the city life.

But amid all this there was another face to Brian; the tough exterior was okay to portray, but it was equally difficult to maintain the privacy of his soft heart. He was always on guard, always. He was so protective about it that no one could see what he felt, what he thought and what he sensed. No one could come inside that heart without his permission. If he showed what he felt, that was it: it would be the end of that chapter.

That's why he could never be in a relationship; he would change his women as he would change his underwear daily. He did not believe in love.

Why was he like that? No one knew. It could be because his mother passed away when he was one and his father never remarried. Brian felt the sense of obligation his father felt towards his son and dead wife, but always thought that it was very selfish, as if his father wanted to make him feel guilty that he was his father's enormous responsibility for which Brian needed to be forever obligated.

However, today was another one of the wild Sundays for Brian and his best mate and assistant, Dan. Along with a group of friends, they'd just come out of a local bar that played jazz until six in the morning. They wanted to walk but the rain and the fatigue in their bodies forced them to take the tram.

Nonchalant as he was, when he passed a plain looking girl with long dark hair, something made Brian turn his head to catch a glimpse of her. She was ordinary looking, yet so extraordinary. For a moment Brian wondered, how could someone ooze so much sexuality being that plain? She had chocolate skin, her brown eyes shining under the thick eyelashes. He noticed from time to time her left cheek created an impression of a dimple, often when she would purse her lips.

He wanted to capture this beauty on his camera. She looked so innocent and yet so wicked. She had the voluptuous body of a woman, yet a sheepish walk of a schoolgirl. She definitely looked out of placc in that tram stop, trying her best to fit into the crowd; she was fidgety, as if she wanted to be aloof. Brian was now standing very close to her; he was reading all this with his curious eyes. Suddenly he felt the urgency of being on guard again.

He took out a cigarette to light and turned away from her face so he could stop this moment for a while. He'd photographed so many faces but not one like hers.

There was a shine and a radiance about her that was so mesmerising. For a while Brian thought about what it would be to touch her and feel her. He was thinking about all this when a soft yet firm voice came charging towards him. 'Do you mind?'

'Sorry!' Brian replied very politely to the chocolate-skinned woman.

She was still not impressed. 'You shouldn't be smoking in a tram stop; it's unlawful.'

He thought she was not only beaming sexuality, but rude like a grumpy young woman. 'You okay, Brian?' Dan, asked him with a curious frown. 'It's okay, Dan, an FOB I guess. This one is a brick short of the cart load,' Brian said to Dan, pointing his index finger to his head. He made sure the woman heard it too. He was excited with this challenge. He wanted to grab her then and take all there was to take from her. The adrenaline was just kicking in for him.

'Hey! Mate, I am bright enough to know that I am not "fresh off the boat" and I am definitely not a grumpy middle aged man smoking his lungs away and forcing others to do the same too. Get a life, dude. I think I can provide you that brick which is short off your head.'

Brian was speechless. When she was annoyed, she made a peculiar face he found captivating. Finally he'd met someone who wouldn't caress his ego; *Finally*, he thought, *here is a woman who doesn't fall easy for looks*. Instead, Brian was succumbing to her. His green eyes were shining and his lips broke into a smile. He laughed, winking at her. Others laughed with Brian, some clapped. He ran to follow her.

'Brian, where are you going mate?' Dan screamed from behind.

'I don't know her name!' Still laughing, Brian waved goodbye and Dan exactly knew what was coming.

Once inside the tram, Brian searched for his chocolate-skinned woman. The tram was bulging with people clinging close to each other, but he managed to pass through all the irritated people of the morning rush. There she was, sitting next to an elderly woman by the window. He kept staring at her; he wanted to get her attention but she seemed to be lost in her own thoughts. With one hand on the handle for support, he searched his coat pocket for a pen. He took out his pad and scribbled. When done, he nudged the elderly woman and made an apologetic face, asking in sign language if she could pass it to the lady beside her. The elderly woman was neither happy nor irritated to do this for him.

Meera turned to the elderly woman, smiling when she was handed her the note, although she was quite surprised. She had no clue that Brian was just standing a few feet away from her.

'Hi, I am Brian. You owe me a name at least. Regards, The Cigarette Offender.'

She couldn't believe what she was reading; she looked straight and then turned to her left; there he was, a bigger smile than before.

'Hi! Do you mind if we have a cup of coffee?' This time Brian was polite.

'Meera, that's my name. I have to be at work now – maybe later.' She smiled for the first time. Her white teeth stood out against her chocolate skin – it was a beautiful smile.

Grabbing the piece of paper from Meera, he quickly scribbled his name and number.

The Date

Meera couldn't believe what had just happened. She was smiling at his wickedness. She had to give it to him: the title of being brave. How could someone so rude be so charming? She agreed to the coffee because of the effort he made to jump on the tram just to give his number to her – not because she thought anything much of him. For the first time, Meera saw how attractive he was. *He is a distraction*, she thought to herself. The piece of paper in her hand with Brian's number did not feel so important anymore; scrunching it with her hand, the piece of paper made its way to the rubbish bin. She nodded with a smile.

The next day she was on her daily route to work, waiting at the same tram stop minding her own business. She looked across the tram stop, recalling yesterday's episode with the stranger who handed her his number. She felt reluctant to be standing there. *What if anyone recognised me, or I cross paths with him again?* Luckily, the cigarette man wasn't there. He became a distant memory.

***

A few weeks later on a Monday, Meera, on her way to work, glanced up to see the overcast sky above, clouds swelling with rain. She looked inside her bag for her pocket umbrella only to be disappointed. She cursed herself, pontificating – what if? But when she looked at her watch, it was already ten to eight. She wouldn't want to risk her manager giving her a pep talk on punctuality. Before the swelled-up clouds broke into heavy pouring rain, taking refuge under the tram stop seemed like a good option.

She stood with her back towards the tram stop, folding her arms across her chest trying to comfort herself from the chilly air, lost in her thoughts, thinking about a valid point for being late to work. Just then she felt a tingling sensation that ran up her spine; someone was too close to her, breathing on her ears, whispering.

'You never called?'

Meera jolted with a fright at the whisperer, as if the cat caught her tongue. She managed, still in a shock, 'O-oh! I thought you were just being polite.'

'I was being polite, but I thought this way I could manage to apologise to you for my rude behaviour.' The cigarette offender now spoke softly and clearly.

Meera felt awkward and tried her best to sound interested in the conversation. 'It's all good, I had already forgotten, I don't see the need for you to apologise to me again.'

It was Brian's turn to smile. 'Then why didn't you call?'

'Was I meant to?' Meera was now trying to hide the fact that she threw away his phone number; her pretence turned into arrogance and trickery.

By now she could see Brian towering over her, as if

his tall broad masculine body was preventing her from escaping him, clenching his teeth that was supposed to be a smile. He tried grabbing Meera's shoulder. She could smell the heavy stench of alcohol under his breath. She managed to walk away from him, smiling.

The dimples on her cheek were enough to electrify Brian once more and he was about to try grabbing her shoulder again when his friend Dan interrupted. 'Excuse my friend for his behaviour; he is in an inebriated state.'

'No I am not, Dan! Do you remember her? The same FOB … err … sorry, excuse me, the girl who cursed me for smoking. Me … Myra!'

'It's *Meera*, not Myra,' Meera corrected him.

Brian cleared his throat and was once again on his best behaviour. 'Dan, this is Meera – Meera, this is Dan. And I am, of course, Brian.'

'Hi Dan! Yes, I know your name Brian.' Meera and Dan exchanged glances on Brian's incorrigible behaviour. Meera rolled her eyes to Dan and shook her head with a disapproving smirk.

'Can I have your phone, please?' Brian asked Meera.

'May I ask why?'

'So I can save my number for you to call me for that coffee.'

'You are very persuasive, aren't you?' Meera could feel herself getting angry. 'Is he always like this, Dan?'

'Only after a couple of beers … give him your number, otherwise we both will be stuck here forever.' Dan looked at Meera with a helpless plea.

'Do you always make the habit of being so overbearing?' she said to Brian.

'And do you always make it a habit of throwing someone's number away when all he wanted was a cup of coffee with you for a sincere apology?'

By now her guilt was showing all over her face; she squeezed her hand to form a fist but instead she pointed out a finger at Brian. Smiling, she said, 'You got me.'

'He is harmless, and seriously – if you want to get on with your day today, just say yes to him.' Dan chuckled at Meera.

By now Meera was slightly embarrassed at her actions and gave him the thumbs up. She searched through her bag for her phone and eventually she took Brian's number. She thought that would be the end of it.

'Text me!' Brian was now challenging her.

'Is he serious?' She looked at Dan, who was now an active participant in this game. He nodded back at her, smiling.

Looking up at the sky that was now pouring with rain, she laughed. 'I can't believe I'm doing this.' She sent a text saying, 'Hi'.

Brian smiled and was very quick in responding with a text. 'Coffee, this afternoon?'

'How annoying are you?' Meera laughed and it was soon all a joke for the three of them as they began chatting about the cigarette incident the other day.

'Well! Gentlemen, I have to go now, I already missed two trams,' Meera said, signalling to a tram that was fast approaching.

'Sure,' Brian replied.

When the doors of the tram closed behind Meera, she could see Brian getting soaked in the rain while making a sign of a phone with his fingers; he signed 'call me'. Meera lowered her head and laughed.

It's just a coffee, she thought. She was once again drawn to his attractiveness; this time, however, it was not about his physical attributes but his persuasiveness, and to how he remembered her after all these weeks.

She took out her phone and sent Brian a text. 'Say six at the Ferris wheel down by the waterfront?'

The reply was sent with a smiley face and, 'Sure, see you at six then.'

***

'Lalita, Lalita. You wouldn't believe what happened today.' Meera told the whole story to her friend.

Lalita was not impressed. 'What a loser. Don't tell me you are going. What happens if he wants to have sex on the first date?'

'Come on Lalita, shut up. Let's not discuss this anymore. Help me with what I should wear.'

Lalita was not at all happy with her friend's choice of date. She quickly made her exit.

'Oh well! Whatever,' Meera whispered under her breath and looked herself in the mirror.

She touched her long black hair, which shone with the fading winter sun. Standing on an angle in front of the mirror, she caught a glimpse of herself; for the first time in many years she was looking at herself with judging eyes. She thought what it would have been like losing a bit of fat around the belly. She touched her face. What it would be like adding a bit of colour to the dark skin, some pink eyeshadow or a bit of lipstick?

She touched her bony neck; in soft strokes, she made her way down to her chest, touching her breasts. She was slightly aroused. She felt curious of this new sensation and wanted to explore a bit more, so she let it go and became more adventurous. She rubbed her belly and the side of her ribcage, hesitant to explore further. Feeling guilty, she looked away from the mirror. She touched her vagina for the first time in twenty-seven years. She rubbed her fingers gently on it, closing her eyes; she wanted to imagine the possibilities. She wondered what it would be like to feel a man's groin there. Why was she thinking that? Because it reminded her of how she'd forgotten to take care of herself, or how she has kept herself away from all these deadly, guilty pleasures? All she needed now was to open her chastity belt. The key was in her head.

Was Brian so attractive that he made her wicked with such arousing thoughts, or was her virginity killing her slowly without the knowledge of knowing lust? Who thought that a man like Brian would arouse such sexual fantasies within her? Or was it just another stab of loneliness? She quickly let her hands go as she felt guilty of all these conflicting thoughts.

Lalita jumped from the mirror behind – as if watching Meera's every move. 'Look, I told you it's a bad idea to meet this guy.'

'I am going to prove you wrong, Lalita. Can you just leave me alone and stop making me feel nervous?'

Lalita couldn't help but laugh loudly and with contempt. Before leaving Meera alone inside the room she said, 'Suffer, Meera! Suffer in the hands of love. I won't be there and no one will be there, not even that idol of Lord Krishna you carry with such dignity. So go and suffer in the hands of Brian, rot in sex and rot in love. You will be disowned.'

'You will disown me? Just disappear for a while and let me think this through my way.' Meera turned her back, signalling for Lalita to leave the room without any further conversation.

***

Brian was waiting in the café, neatly dressed in his smart denim jacket and smelling of his infamously expensive cologne. He'd shaved his stubble and the white shirt under his denim jacket brought out his green eyes. They were sparkling with anxiousness. He kept looking at Meera's message: 'See you at six'. He was too old for this game, and was getting anxious over whether she would come or not. It was, after all, a challenge for Brian. The challenge was not to outdo a smart women like her; he set himself this challenge to outdo himself, for what he is always damned to be known as 'the man who cannot fall in love'.

Patiently waiting, he smiled at the waitress to order a glass of wine. He thought that would calm him down. He looked at the big clock for the fourth time and it was just 5.40. He was early and smiled at himself. 'What am I doing?' he heard himself saying. He thought he wanted this; he wanted to win and be accepted for what he was. Meera could give him that, if he could only look beyond his own insecurities and value what would be given to him. He was frustrated and suddenly angry with Meera, blaming her for being that person he always wanted to fall in love with. He cursed her silently.

Just when he was planning how he would get rid of Meera if need be, he felt someone tapping at his shoulder. He turned back to look at a smiling Meera. He got up to give her a kiss on her cheek; she had a clean fresh smell that was overpowered by his own cologne. He felt the warmth of her cheeks. He did his best to hide his excitement.

She sat opposite him; he saw that her eyelids had some kind of a pink eyeshadow and the eyes were smudged with kohl. Her lips were glossed pink. Brian tried his best not to laugh but just smiled at the effort she went to for this date. He thought that made her look stunning – but he still preferred the Meera he saw in the morning without makeup.

'I have to apologise for my behaviour in the morning. I sometimes get carried away with things I am passionate about. If you haven't noticed, I not only value feminism but also protect myself from narcissism.' Meera said this with a big apologetic laugh.

Brian laughed with her. She was not only smart but was witty. This was all so interesting for him. 'The modern woman from the east is, after all, not a myth.'

'Be careful where you are going with this, Brian, you might sound racist.' Meera raised her eyebrows with a smile.

He couldn't help but wink at her, signalling at the waiter to order some wine. 'I wouldn't dare that challenge again.' He thought she had him down pat on this one; she exactly knew how to excite him.

'What do you do?'

'You mean what I do for a living?' Brian asked, taking a sip from his glass. 'I am a photographer; I sometimes travel the world searching for a story, or a story just happens to search for me. You can say I'm a journalist, as I travel around with famous journalists … so yeah! I am one too.'

'You are very modest.' Meera was now teasing him. 'If I was you I would be openly proud and say that with arrogance. Like I am about to, before you ask what I do. I am a proud microbiologist – only a junior consultant at this stage, but one day I will be a *famous* microbiologist.' Meera stretched her neck upwards and raised her left eyebrow to snob Brian.

Brian laughed. 'Got it, next time I shall add that arrogance but will never be able to say it with such confidence. You know, not only do you make it sound so easy but it also makes you look so attractive.' Being suddenly aware of what he just said put him on his guard again. He changed the subject and said to Meera it would be a good idea to order some food. 'They make some fantastic burgers here.'

She sensed that the Brian she met in the morning was slightly more formal in the evening. *I have to make it easy for him*, Meera thought to herself. 'Thanks for the compliment – and sure, I would love a burger,' she replied with enthusiasm, as if she never heard the word 'burger' before. She was trying her best to hide her blushed cheeks with this sudden frankness from Brian. What she just said or did – was it all just her, or was she oozing all Lalita's confidence? Meera paused to think for a short while. Maybe she was just starting to like him.

The evening went on smoothly from there; they both not only admired each other's perception on life but they were comfortable in each other's company. They both came to know they were born as an only child, but the only difference was that Meera had so much love from her family, which was not only overprotective but sometimes suffocating.

Brian, on the other hand, despised his father as it always reminded him how his father would blame him for ... everything. *The turn of the glass*, Brian thought. After a dozen beers Brian's father would scream at him for leading a lonely and sloppy life. He would bring up all the money he spent on Brian, feeding him, clothing him and giving him a roof over his head. Brian would hide under the bed until his father's alcoholic fit stopped. When he heard the last can of beer being thrown at the wall, it was a cue for Brian to clean up the mess and take his father to bed. Brian felt sorry for him, sometimes hating him to a degree that he wished his father was dead.

Strangely enough, when his father did die, Brian thought he would be happy that there would be no more alcohol tantrums, no more blame games – but in fact, Brian was sad as now there was no family or home to go back to.

Hearing his love for the camera, she began to understand his passion and was secretly admiring the creative person behind all that arrogance.

After dinner, they both walked outside to the chill winter air. It was time to say goodbye to each other but Brian was not ready yet. He pulled Meera close to him and he could sense she was slightly shaking. She thought he could almost hear her heart racing. He searched her deep brown eyes as if searching for himself there. *Oh! Yes! He is good at this*, Meera thought.

He lowered his head and gave a soft kiss on Meera's lips. This caught Meera by surprise; she had no reaction to give to Brian, although he was not at all looking for one.

'Do you have the habit of kissing people on their first date?'

'Was that a kiss? It was just my acknowledgement of saying I had a great evening,' Brian said nodding with a smile. 'Do dinner with me at my house, I will cook.'

'Really, can you cook? So am I bringing my own dinner just in case?' Meera said that quite seriously.

'No! That shouldn't be a problem; I have a nice pizza place just around the corner if all goes wrong.' They both laughed.

By now Meera was comfortable with him; she gave him a quick kiss on his cheek. She was not that tall but tall enough to reach for Brian's cheeks. She smelled the overpowering cologne on his neck, which was a relief from the morning's stale smell of alcohol. For a brief moment she wanted to be intoxicated with his cologne, keep it hidden in a safe place in her memory; whenever she was lonely she would travel back in time to tonight, to him and to everything attached to him.

Meera felt aroused at every thought of him. 'Was Lalita right about all this?' She looked at Brian and gave him a smile of helplessness.

The Rejection

The suppressed feelings, the self-pity. Sitting in a corner alone – slightly ashamed, slightly proud of his achievements – he looked at the empty wine glass. He felt empty and hollow just like it. The only difference was that he was not made of glass, but still more fragile than ever before, waiting to be shattered into a million pieces if touched by just a drop of love.

What would become of him if Meera fell in love with him? Would he be able to match or withstand the strength of her love? Or would he be doomed forever?

The deliberate short kisses, the odd strokes of her hair, the feel of her breath, the softness of her face, those eyes of Meera's from which he wanted to see the world from. He was making it all impossible for himself. Would he die if he made love to her? Just a glimpse of himself making love to her tormented him every day. While walking, in the shower, having a coffee or on assignments, he would fantasise about it. Meera was like a forbidden fruit: he couldn't have her, touch her, feel her – he had to let go of her, as if just one touch could ruin her innocence forever.

He couldn't see himself or anyone with her. Her posture, the continuous nodding of her head, her charming sense of humour – and her pretence of knowing the difference between still and tap water if asked by a waiter, and how beautifully she would hide that by feigning confidence. Brian was afraid of losing himself to her.

'Say six at the Ferris wheel down by the waterfront?' Brian read the text that Meera sent to him. He flicked through his phone for photos of Meera and stumbled across another photo he'd almost forgotten. His heart sank, his mouth was dry, and his hands searched for the empty wine glass.

'How can I forget?' Pouring another glass of wine, he took a small sip then threw his phone on the table. 'Damn you, Hannah! Damn! You!' Cursing under his breath, he smashed the wine glass on the wooden floor. 'Fuck! What am I doing?' He closed his eyes only to see a vision of Hannah flashing in front of him.

***

'Brian, could you pass me the stapler please?' Emily smiled. 'Don't you think this internship is a killer? It's so taxing. Don't know when they will make us permanent.'

Emily continued her whining while Brian kept looking at his computer, handing Emily the stapler. 'Thanks!' Emily replied.

Brian was ignoring Emily, watching his computer screen, waiting for the office communicator to flash a reply. He was getting agitated and impatient. He turned away from his screen to look outside the window, as if waiting for a miracle to happen. He counted in his mind – one, two, three – and turned back on the screen again. Still no response. Giving up, he was just about to join in Emily's whining when he saw a reply from Hannah: 'We are on.'

An ecstatic Brian said, 'Welcome, Emily! Don't think too much of the job – even the guy from the café downstairs can be a journalist. You just concentrate on the story. See you tomorrow.'

Brian grabbed his stuff to rush towards the door. Emily rolled her eyes, making a face at him. 'You are a douchebag, Brian Johnson.'

'I know, Emily, but you will still come to me for my advice.' Brian laughed, waved his goodbye and ran to catch the lift.

Outside his office, he could see Hannah waiting with some of their office mates. She signalled with her eyes at Brian to walk away. Brian knew the daily routine. He would wait for his boss outside the office and then follow her until she reached the car park, where he would quietly slip in the back seat of her car. If anyone saw them, 'Hannah is giving me a lift,' would be his response.

'Your place or mine?' Hannah asked once they were both in the car and pulling out of her parking spot. Brian was quiet, looking at her in the rear view mirror. 'What's wrong?' she asked.

'I am tired of this! Hannah, when are we going to stop meeting like this, hiding from people?'

Hannah pulled over to the side in the parking lot. Brian knew she wanted him to sit next to her now. Fixing her hair, she turned to Brian to give him one of her most amazing smiles. She knew how to make him go weak on his knees with her perfume and her smile. Every time she smiled, her cheeks would break into dimples and her soft brown eyes would shine under those thick eyelashes. There was no sign of wrinkles around her face for anyone to guess her age. According to Brian, she was ageless. He was mesmerised by her beauty and brains.

She sprayed some of the perfume on her long neck that ignited a mixed smell of blackberries, vanilla and cedar wood. It was always very sensual on her dark skin; even a tiny drop was enough to ignite Brian. He was always captivated by her voice and her smell. Brian grabbed her arms and gave her a passionate kiss.

'Every time you do that, I just want to grab you and make you mine,' Brian said.

'You know this is not forever, you know that right?' Pushing Brian away from her, she drove.

'Ouch! That hurts, Hannah! Do you always have to be blunt? I know this age difference. I will never jeopardise your reputation at work. Let's go to my place.' Brian smiled.

***

Hannah was Brian's boss, and much older than him. She hired Brian for his amazing work but was not attracted to him on first sight. During an office chit-chat one day everyone was sharing their photos from their younger days when Brian, being the office joker and never hesitant to show his frizzy hair in a jumpsuit from his country days, made quite an impression with his photos. Brian's phone passed to Emily, then to Dan and then all the way through everyone; Emily, who couldn't stop laughing, then ran to show it to their boss.

'Is that you, Brian?' Hannah asked him with a surprised look. He ran across to grab the phone from her.

In a very sexy flirtatious voice she whispered into Brian's

ear, 'Well! Well!' Her short curvy body kneeling on to him, he could smell her perfume overpowering his cologne. He would always know she was around the office; it was not any magic, it was just Hannah's perfume.

He was wondering, what would it be like to feel her? 'Add me on your Facebook.'

'What a preposterous idea, Brian Johnson! I am your boss, personal life is strictly non-negotiable.' Hannah winked at Brian. She took the phone from his hand and added herself.

***

'How's things, Hannah?'

'Look who's come out to play at night?' Hannah replied to Brian's text.

Brian was alarmed at the text. *Am I being flirtatious? It's just a text. 'How's things?'* Brian thought to himself. Five minutes later, the phone buzzed another text from Hannah.

'Finish the story and if it's published … I will cook for you.'

Wow! Brian thought to himself. He replied, 'It's done!''

***

'Well done, mate.' Dan patted Brian's back, throwing the newspaper in front of him. The *Sunday Magazine*'s headline story was of a man imprisoned for killing his lover. The heading of the article was, 'Story of a jilted lover' and the by-line read 'Brian Johnson'.

'Thanks, mate! Where's Hannah?' Brian asked Dan.

Winking back at Brian, Dan replied, 'Can't you smell her yet?'

They both laughed but soon were interrupted by Hannah. 'Let's have a huddle everyone.' She looked striking in her red dress; the colour sat well over her olive skin. He couldn't stop looking at her. Noticing this, Dan nudged him with an elbow and whispered in his ears, 'You have got the dengue fever, mate.'

The huddle was meant for Brian to be recognised for his published story. When all the applause ended and everyone back at their seats, Brian quietly went over to Hannah and whispered, 'So now will you cook for me?'

Hannah smiled, making sure those dimples did their work. 'Go back to your desk now,' Hannah ordered Brian.

Brian frowned at her and did what he was ordered to do. Five minutes later he received a text from Hannah: 'Your address?'

Brian couldn't stop smiling. In his thrill he sent his address on the office communicator and got a response from Hannah. 'Not this medium. I prefer text.'

***

They met at Brian's place that night. Hannah brought with her a casserole of lamb shanks. 'Wow! That looks like a real dinner; I have just the thing to go with that.' Brian pulled out a bottle of red wine from his pantry.

'Well! As I presumed, what would a bachelor have in his pantry other than food? What about some scotch?' Hannah asked.

'No problem,' was the reply.

As they sat down to eat their dinner with a glass of scotch each in their hand, Hannah sat close to Brian on the only sofa he had. He lived in a studio apartment with a bed, sofa, fridge, microwave, writing desk, table – and a big fifty inch plasma TV.

'Can I be frank with you?' Hannah asked.

'Sure. By the way, these are the best lamb shanks I have had in years.'

Smiling back at Brian, Hannah continued. 'Thanks, but can I ask you something? What if I put forward a proposition for you?'

Brian frowned at Hannah.

'What if we have just an exchange of physical transaction between us, nothing emotional, purely sexual?' Hannah was looking straight into his eyes.

Brian was not shocked at all; he was wishing for something on these lines to happen. Taking Hannah's plate from her hand and tossing both their plates on the table, he grabbed Hannah to kiss her passionately.

***

They stood in Hannah's kitchen, looking at each other in silence.

'The secret rendezvous are getting out of control,' Brian finally said, looking at Hannah with anxious eyes. He wanted to talk to her more but then the soft whisk of her finger on his lips made it impossible. He kissed it back.

'We have been doing this almost six months. Do you think we can take this further? Is that what you were trying to say, Brian? To make this more than just an office fling?' Hannah smiled at Brian, convincing him that it just could be a possibility.

He grabbed Hannah's arm, her face close to his, to search for any answers. Hannah couldn't hold any longer and cracked, laughing. 'I just loved the look on your face. I am joking, Brian Johnson, we cannot take this further. I don't see us together.'

'Thank God you made it simple for me, Hannah. I was just getting worried.' Brian laughed. But before he could continue to make it all a big joke, Hannah's face turned serious.

'I am pregnant, Brian.'

'You are joking right?' Brian looked at Hannah. She just stared at Brian without any emotions. Her face hardened. 'Look at your face!' Brian laughed.

'No! Brian, I am not joking at all, I am three weeks pregnant.'

Brian just looked at her for a long time, before gently stroking her red hair. 'It's going to be alright, we can do this together. We both can – I can bring up the child.'

'You are kidding me, Brian. Why would you want to do that?' Hannah laughed.

'I know this is not the right time … but then, there will not be any appropriate time than this. I love you Hannah, will you marry me?'

Hannah just looked at Brian and laughed again. 'What a preposterous idea, Brian – marry you? Let alone the fact I don't love you.' She stormed into the kitchen, making herself look busy.

Brian turned white; those words seemed to have sucked the life out of him. It wasn't the fact that she said no to marriage, but her disapproval, the fact she didn't love him – it was not what he wanted to hear. Slowly walking towards her, he could feel his legs heavy and the earth below sinking away. *Christ! Dig a hole and take me alive*, he thought.

'Hannah!' Brian whispered.

'Please, Brian, I wanted to tell you but hadn't the courage … but getting pregnant was the last thing on my mind. I love someone else. If you have any more self-respect you will leave now.'

Brian felt his heart compressing with a sharp pain. *Heart attack*, he thought, but actually it was the pain of not being loved. He felt his mouth dry, his face warm and his eyes become cloudy with tears. He walked towards the door glancing at Hannah as he whispered, 'I did love you, you know.'

Brian walked into the empty lobby of Hannah's building, hearing himself sobbing. He ran towards his car, trying to be as discreet as possible. Once inside his car he locked himself and let the floodgates open – the sobs turned into louder shrieks of crying.

***

He rubbed his tears and started gathering the shattered wine glass pieces from the floor. It was almost two years since that day in Hannah's apartment and it has been three years since the night of his first date with Meera. They would often meet during the weekend, whenever Brian was available in the city. Sometimes the weekend coffees would turn into weekday lunches. It was always the same every time. Meera would be waiting in a corner of a café, sipping a cup of coffee.

Today, Brian made a different but deliberate choice. He took the back alley to enter via the kitchen door; it was not a problem as he knew the owner, who was also the chef.

'Poached eggs on sourdough with avocados or beans? What coffee, piccolo or flat white?'

Brian nodded in approval. 'All good, except the coffee. Could you make me a double scotch?'

'Sure! Go and take a seat with your friend. I will bring that to you,' the chef responded, confused.

'Is it okay if I just sit here today and have it?' Brian gave him a look of hopelessness. He'd known the chef for a long time; the day he opened the doors, Brian was his first customer. They were friends and Brian gave him a lot of business over the years by being excellent PR for his café. According to Brian, that's what good journalists do when the city goes sparse for good coffee. Brian promoted the café for free – and for that the chef had a huge respect for Brian.

The chef looked at him and did not ask anything more; he made his scotch and took a tray of his food to him. 'Brian, come to my office – you will be more comfortable there.' He hesitated for a while and then looked at him again. 'Trust me, just come.'

Brian followed his chef friend to his office. He switched on the lights to his office. Brian was gobsmacked. The wall had a 100 inch TV on the wall. The entire café was alive in front of him. The CCTV turned into a reality show. Handing him the remote, he flicked at table number twenty-three; Meera was looking straight at him through the TV screen.

The chef said to Brian, 'You will be more comfortable here. I will make sure no one comes in.' He smiled.

'Thank you.' Brian replied.

'Love is a dangerous thing, my friend. It can ignite you with passion or leave you burning forever,' his chef friend said in a sad voice.

Brian heard himself whispering, 'I cannot do this!' He saw in the TV screen that Meera was looking at her watch and outside towards the door, waiting for him. It has been almost an hour; the torture was killing Brian. He took a deep breath and gulped the scotch straight down, his eyes fixed on the TV screen. He ran out the door when he saw Meera leaving.

'Meera, I am here,' Brian screamed at the top of his voice and grabbed her by the arm.

'What's the matter? Why are you in such a rush? I am just going to the ladies. What's the matter?' Meera was not only shocked but also taken back with his preposterous behaviour.

Realising what just happened, Brian was quick to sort himself out. 'I will wait for you outside. Let's go to yours – I will make dinner and we'll talk.'

'Okay, give me a sec, I will meet you outside.'

Meera looked at him, confused – he never asked to go her place.

***

On their way to Meera's house, they stopped at the supermarket to shop for dinner. Meera was amused that Brian would be cooking dinner for her. The menu was nothing exciting, chicken and pasta, but the gesture was incredibly thrilling for her. She quickly made a detour to the bottle shop for a bottle of white wine. 'Wicked!' Brian winked at her.

The thought of having Brian in her apartment was not only a frivolous feeling for Meera but deep down she was intrigued what caused him to decide this. He indeed could sometimes be mysterious. Quickly tossing all these thoughts at the back of her mind, she reached out to help Brian in the kitchen, not wary about Lalita's opinion at all.

'Cheers!' Raising her glass in the air, Meera smiled at Brian, who was dishing the chicken out of the plastic tray into the hot pan. 'Wow! Look at you, here cooking for me. I never thought this day would come, Master Chef.' Meera chuckled.

'Hardly, it's just chicken and pasta – that's all I know, and that's not Italian either.' Brian smiled.

Taking a sip from her glass, Meera was watching Brian very closely. Yes, he was good-looking but that never overly mattered to her; what mattered to her was the careless nudge and touch, the nervous anticipation, him coming to her place cooking, his abruptness. What was this? She shook off her nervousness to better concentrate on the present with him.

'You never speak about your family. I never hear anything about them.'

'My family … well, there is nothing to talk about.' Brian winked at Meera. Quickly changing the subject, Brian mixed the chicken with the pasta and dished it to a bowl. 'The classic is ready.' He handed Meera her bowl.

Meera quickly clicked a photo of him just when Brian was about to put a spoonful of his infamous pasta in his mouth. Brian smiled and was quietly watching her. The wine glass in his hand was making him nervous, but not at all shy of the proposition that he was about to offer Meera.

'It's a good pasta, isn't it?' said Brian. Meera nodded in approval; she was about to say something when Brian interrupted. 'Meera, you are beautiful – what if I have a transaction for you?'

'What do you mean?' Meera looked at him blankly.

'What if we have to have just an exchange of physical transaction between us – nothing emotional, purely sexual?' Brian was watching her more closely now.

Slightly nervous in commenting, Meera gave him a look of frustration. 'What if … if one of us falls in love with the other?'

'It will not happen – live in the moment, Meera.'

'I don't think so Brian, it's not possible.'

There was awkward silence between the two for a good minute or two, when finally Brian decided to excuse himself to go to the bathroom. Meera felt hurt; she didn't expect that Brian would make such an odd proposition.

She took a sip of her wine, waiting for him to come out of the bathroom and say how ridiculous he was being. She was angry, and she was scared for the first time, as if he did not know Brian at all.

Her thoughts were interrupted when Brian appeared again, standing next to her. The awkward silence was too much for Meera; carefully manipulating the wine glass slipping from her sweaty fingers, she tried to smile at him when suddenly she was engulfed by his strong hands. Brian grabbed her by the waist and pulled her closer to his face. There was only silence and Meera's heart beating furiously. Brian lowered his head and kissed Meera on her lips. He pushed with his tongue to open Meera's lips and taste the sweetness that he was so eagerly waiting all these years. Meera closed her eyes; as scared as she felt moments ago, the adrenaline kicked in with his sweet tongue teasing her lips, caressing her mouth, questioning her, pleading to her to lose herself in the moment.

Brian quietly took a shy, shivering Meera to the bedroom. His hands all over her body, rubbing her back. His fingers slid inside her blouse and reached for her bra straps. Meera wanted to say no but was helpless. She was in a trance. She wanted it now.

Suddenly she remembered what Lalita had said to her earlier. She quickly pushed Brian's hands away but the temptation to be with a man was something that she wanted to explore. Meera quietly closed her eyes and took Brian's hands in hers. She wanted to explore and discover her sexual side; was Brian just a medium or was it her excuse to have sex?

She moved her head towards Brian's ear and caressed it with her lips. She was careful in her explicit desires but definitely not subtle. Meera took Brian's hands to her breasts, hinting for him to open her bra. She quietly nibbled his ears and stroked the back of his ears with her tongue. The sensation was enough for Brian to take over Meera. He grabbed both of her hands, kissing her, taunting her with his tongue. She wasn't sure what would come next; she was excited and wanted more.

At first Meera was nervous but slowly she began to remove her clothes, one by one. She reached her hands out to open Brian's shirt but he grabbed them and kissed them gently. Softly pushing her to her own bed, making sure she was comfortable in her position until he removed his clothes. She was shaking nervously under Brian's strong physical presence. Sensing this, he brought Meera closer to his chest, kissing her – he stroked her cheeks and then slowly gently pushed himself inside her. She screamed when he entered her, slowly pushing his hardness away from her. She tried to tell something to Brian but their eyes met only acknowledge that they both wanted this deeply. He kissed her and went harder, his eyes fixed on her. Those deep green eyes were so intense for Meera that she did not realise she was bleeding.

Brian pulled away, kissing her shoulders. 'I'm sorry … I didn't know it's your first time.'

Meera smiled. 'It's okay, I am glad it was you.' Meera sat herself up and kissed Brian. Her tongue teasing Brian, she took his hardness in her hand and placed it firmly inside her. Meera screamed in ecstasy. Brian held her, softly kissing her arms; he gazed into her eyes and smiled at her. Meera smiled back at him. The night was sedated by their passions.

***

Resting Meera's head on the pillow, Brian gently put the covers on her body. He watched her peaceful face deep in sleep, and kissed her forehead. Slowly opening her eyes, Meera looked at Brian with a smile. 'What time is it? I must have dozed off.'

'You looked very peaceful,' Brian said smiling. 'Come on, get up. I want to show you something that involves a bit of water.' Meera frowned at him. 'You don't mind getting your head wet?' Brian quizzed her.

'Uh?' was all she could say.

Taking Meera by his hand, he led her to the bathroom. Pushing her hair back on the side of her ears, he kissed her softly on her mouth. He looked at her for a long time and slowly whispered, 'I will be the best you ever had.'

Meera smiled shyly, correcting Brian. 'You mean I will ever have.' They both chuckled.

The warm water splashing on each other's skin, their hands candidly touching each other's body, they were not shy to see each other in light. They not only felt secure and welcoming in each other's touch, kisses, smiles and laughter – but they both felt as if there will not be a tomorrow.

They made love again; they both knew it was something they had together.

***

Zipping his pants, Brian kissed Meera on her forehead. 'I will leave you at peace now.'

'Won't you stay the night?' Meera asked him with a surprised look.

Quickly changing the subject, Brian persuaded Meera to stay in bed as he would see himself out.

'Wait! I will come, Brian.' She quickly slipped into her bathrobe. She grabbed Brian's hands and whispered softly to his ears, 'Thank you!' She tried kissing Brian but he was hesitant – he tried to pull himself away.

'No worries! Don't you think we have done enough kissing for the night?'

That took Meera by surprise. Was she being too sensitive? She paused for a while.

'I will leave you in peace now.' He kissed Meera on the forehead. They both looked at each other for a while before Brian stepped outside.

The outside air was comforting; Brian lit a cigarette and sat on the bench in the park outside Meera's building. From where he sat he could see Meera's bedroom window. He stared at the window, light still coming through her room; he felt a sense of comfort knowing that she was still awake. *Am I scared of being alone, or is the company of Meera an easy way of forgetting my messed up head with Hannah?* he thought. He stared at Meera's window until lights went off – yet again, despair and loneliness seemed to take over his mind.

***

'Here is my resignation.' Brian tried to be as professional as possible. It took him a week to come to the office to face her again.

Hannah looked at Brian very closely. 'Don't do this, Brian! Don't let this ruin your career. Let's discuss this over a coffee. Come on now.'

'God! How can all this be so easy for you, Hannah? It seems to you that nothing happened, like *nothing*.' Brian could hear his voice rise.

Hannah stood up. Grabbing Brian by the arm she literally dragged him to the lift before the whole office could come to know about their fling. 'Let's talk. I like you but I don't love you, Brian.'

'Yes, yes, you told me that, why are you repeating yourself? The child that you are carrying is mine, have you thought about that?' Brian found it amusing to make her guilty.

The whole way to the café they both were quiet. Hannah still looked calm. When they took a seat at one of the café's tables, they faced each other in silence pretending to be nice.

Finally Hannah spoke. 'I know it's not easy for you and it had been equally difficult for me too. I just wanted you to know I have not kept the baby. I am sorry; I think this was the best thing to do. Please forgive me.' She was crying as she reached her hand out to Brian for comfort.

Brian looked at Hannah with disgust and pushed her hand away, gulping his tears; he stood up, pushing his chair away. As he walked off he could hear Hannah screaming. 'This is best for me – for you and for us. Brian, wait!'

The Wedding

Meera looked at herself in the mirror, shining in a red gold sari with gold ornaments around her neck. She tried to smile – at least, she pretended to smile, but she couldn't. It was hard. All she could hear was laughter around her and the television in the background blaring with the news of war about to break on the border of the country.

A young girl in her teens or early twenties screamed on top of her voice, 'Can someone stop the news, it's so depressing! Please, could someone put some music?' All the younger cousins and relatives flocked around the TV remote to switch channels, each telling the other what is more appropriate for a wedding song in a music video.

While these shenanigans were going on with the younger crowd, the older women were not far behind, each outdoing the other in praising Meera over how beautiful she looked; some also praised her soon-to-be husband. They were all whispering to each other, 'Will he leave his bride and go to the war, or will it be beauty before duty? We'll see!' They all roared in shrieks of laughter.

The noise was comforting to her, as the loneliness within her was struggling to understand all this. Lalita was beside her; Meera just wanted five minutes to be with her.

'Look, the groom's car is here!' someone screamed, standing by the window. Hearing this, the women in Meera's room gathered around the window like a pack of wolves to catch a glimpse of him.

'Oh! Meera, he is so handsome! You are so lucky. He is not only good-looking but is filthy rich; you have all the luck, my girl.'

'Thank you!' Meera replied politely. She was getting very uncomfortable with the whole scenario. She looked at the idol of Lord Krishna next to her and closed her eyes.

She quickly jolted as she felt someone touching her shoulder; she turned to see Mrs Sen nodding her head. 'Come, dear, Vikramaditya is here. It's time you speak to him in person,' Mrs Sen said softly to Meera, sensing how anxious her daughter was.

Meera was always self-conscious when she spoke to Vikramaditya; she chose her words very carefully, as she did not want anything relating to Brian to surface up. The hurt was too much for Meera. Brian was constantly in her mind. The day the alliance proposal came to her parents, Meera couldn't refuse. It was not because she couldn't refuse her parents' decision or trust theirs; instead she thought it was for the best to put her past behind.

Her introducing herself to Vikramaditya was mellow; he, on the other hand, was the opposite. He was not only charismatic but had all the awareness of asking the right questions. He was assertive but not cunning, firm but gentle; he was funny but still spoke sense. Vikramaditya was a military man – not that he joined the army to have any credentials or medals for self-gratification. His father was one of the wealthiest, most well-respected men in the city. After his father's death Vikramaditya was asked to look after the business, which he not only did poorly but painfully. Whatever he did, he remained unsatisfied. He missed the adrenaline rush of an army guy and sitting in an office doing numbers bored him.

Before everything went downhill, Vikramaditya's mother had to take charge. Realising where her son's passion was, she decided to set him free from the mundane routine of an office job. She made him promise that all would be fair if he gave her a daughter-in-law. He was forever grateful for his mother for understanding him well enough to free him from something that he was not at all ready for. He wanted to take his chances and was ready to take a shot at this, thinking he might fall in love with this woman.

On the other hand, Meera knew this was it. She made her choice and it had to work.

***

The ritual was simple but the celebrations were elaborate. The bride and the groom take their first step to tie their nuptial knot around the fire god. According to Hindu custom, the fire god is most auspicious to witness a marriage. The father gives away his daughter for the groom to take her responsibilities, for better or for worse.

Vikramaditya stood there waiting for his bride Meera, who was carried by all her uncles on a wooden plank, where she sat covering her eyes with two betel leaves; this was known as the first sighting of the bride and bridegroom. As soon as she removed the leaves from her eyes, Vikramaditya winked at her. Meera chuckled and her first impression of him somewhat reminded her of Brian. She quickly scolded herself – this was not the right time. The Sanskrit hymns were going on the background as the priest called for them to take their first walk around the fire as husband and wife.

Meera was trying to fight back her tears but the smoke from the fire was not helping; she had to let go of the tears. As they sat together for the *sindoor* (vermilion) to be put into her forehead, Meera closed her eyes to reflect on her memories of Brian for the last time.

***

The celebrations went on for the rest of the night. When the bride and the bridegroom were finally through with the customs, Meera was whisked away to her room to change for the reception.

Once alone in her room, Meera looked at the idol of Krishna, praying for strength.

Lalita, who was just standing across the mirror, spoke. 'You are happy now? Look how much he is like Brian – wait till he tries to come close to you. What will you do then? Let him know that you are still in love with Brian? What will you do, Meera?'

'Lalita, give me space … I cannot think now and I surely don't want to think about this right now. Why don't you just disappear? It's the best thing that you can do right now. You just find an amazing way to hurt me at the right time. I don't need you. Just go away and bother someone else.'

There was a knock at the door, which made Lalita quickly run away.

'Meera, you ready? Everyone is waiting downstairs.' Mrs Sen asked politely.

Meera wiped her tears. Quickly fixing her makeup, she screamed, 'Give me five minutes, maa.'

As soon as Mrs Sen walked in, she could sense something was not right. 'You are happy with this arrangement?' Mrs Sen quizzed her.

'Why is everyone so bothered about how happy I am? You, Lali … never mind.'

'Lali? Who's that, Meera? Is Lalita here?'

'As I told you maa, never mind. Yes, I am happy – if I wasn't happy, why would I say to you I am ready?'

'Meera, since you have come back you have been quite … is there something you want to tell me? Is there someone else in your life?'

Realising what her mother had sensed, she quickly had to change the subject. She smiled. 'There is nothing maa, you just overthink too much. Good you are here, you can help me with the sari.'

'Okay, as long as you are not lying to yourself to make me happy.'

'Come on maa, why I shouldn't be happy? Please, it's getting late, please help me with the sari.'

Meera smiled and hugged her mother. They both got lost into talking, forgetting of what was spoken.

***

The reception ended well, and the last guests left at five in the morning. Meera and Vikramaditya left soon after. Usually the reception is given by the groom's family but Mr Sen and Vikramaditya's mother decided to host the same night as a collaborative gesture. Vikramaditya's mother decided to have a small cocktail party the next day just for close family and friends.

Once at Vikramaditya's house, Meera felt scared and alone for the very first time. She did not shed a tear on her send-off. She just hugged her parents and close friends. She thought that deciding not to speak to Lalita at that moment was the best decision she ever made.

Vikramaditya's mother waited at the gate with her daughter and a few relatives. They did the customary rituals of welcoming the bride and after that she was quickly whisked off to Vikramaditya's room.

'Make her comfortable, Vikram … give her abundance of love but be firm.' She squeezed Vikramaditya's hand. Like an obedient child, he assured his mother with a nod. 'Teach her how the wives in this household are expected to behave,' she continued.

'Mother, I think Meera should be as what she is, I don't want to get into your petticoat government politics. To me she is my friend and my wife,' Vikramaditya whispered in annoyance at his mother's comment. She looked at him, disapproving with a wry smile.

***

Meera looked around the room. Everything looked so different. There were photographs of him wearing his army uniform and medals, with his mother. Everything was so pristine. His uniform hanging next to his wardrobe, his shoes immaculately arranged as if he knew what to wear during the week. She looked around to get familiar with her surroundings but was finding it difficult to cope. She couldn't breathe.

She could only hear Brian's voice. 'Meera!'

She closed her ears and ran outside to the balcony.

The Widow-maker

Meera felt as if she was being watched; she turned back and saw some movement around the house. Quickly she gathered her wits and rushed inside the bedroom. To her surprise there was not a soul; quickly glancing across the room, her eyes stopped at Vikramaditya's table. She saw a bouquet of red roses and a portrait of Lord Krishna, underneath a card that said, 'To my Meera for her Krishna. Vikram.'

It not only touched Meera, but she was surprised he remembered how she spoke to him about her devotion to Krishna. The gold lining around Krishna's lips made the portrait shine with laughter.

'Did you like it?' Vikramaditya came behind the doors where he was hiding, which made her jump out of her skin. Meera turned around to see a smiling man beaming morning rays of sunshine through him. He was glowing gold and Meera was taken back with this sight. Was this a heavenly message that was being delivered by Krishna? Is this the truth and the rest was all a lie? Meera felt sad at this sudden thought.

'Yes,' she said, 'thank you Vikram, that is very thoughtful of you.'

'I didn't know what would be an appropriate wedding gift.' Meera smiled at this comment. 'Can I give you a hug, Meera?'

Meera felt nervous. How would another man's arm feel around her? How would she react? Would her body betray her? Without giving it a second thought, she said yes.

Very cautious of her response, Vikram walked to her very stealthily. Trying not to make it awkward for either of them, he took Meera's hands gently and kissed them. Meera froze.

Vikram's big manly hug overshadowing her petite body was enough for her; she didn't feel the need react to anything. She succumbed to his affection. Everything seemed alright.

For the first time Meera saw him closely. He was not a handsome man to her, but there was something about him that made him look very attractive. When he smiled, Meera could see the shine in his warm affectionate eyes. His slight grey hair along with his distinguished voice made him feel like a perfect gentleman. But for Meera, the present warmth of his hug made Meera secure. She smiled.

From the corner of her eye she could see the television broadcasting news of the war that people thought had been averted. Fresh images of fighter jets and soldiers around the border sent a chilling sensation through Meera's spine. The warm hug of Vikram that made her secure a while ago wasn't enough for her. She held Vikram's arms tightly like a little child.

Vikram, totally unaware of Meera's emotion, responded with a tight embrace.

***

Days went to months, months to a year. Meera was feeling settled in her married life. Most days she would keep to herself in her room, writing songs of Krishna or speaking to Lalita. Her mother-in-law thought she'd married her son to a religious fanatic but her self-doubt would end whenever she asked Meera to join her for any social gatherings. Everybody just loved her. She was witty and a wealth of knowledge if there was a discussion on any agenda. Vikramaditya's mother only liked her daughter-in-law through others' opinions of Meera.

But secretly Meera would thank this boost of confidence to Vikram. They emerged as good friends; she would speak for hours about their deepest secrets. They spoke about Brian and Vikram acknowledged everything about the relationship. He even gave her time; they would only exchange a physical relationship on her terms, when she would be ready.

One day, while they were sitting in the balcony sipping tea, Meera asked Vikramaditya a question that she wanted to for a long time. 'Tell me, if anything is to happen … if a war would break out … what am I supposed to do?'

'If I were never to return again, you will know what to do. Your Krishna will be there, you will ask him.' Vikramaditya smiled, rubbing his fingers on Meera's hair.

Every morning, Vikram would leave a bunch of roses from the garden, an idol of Lord Krishna and a letter for her. She had collected three hundred miniature idols of Lord Krishna over the year – Vikram had to build a small cabinet for her.

***

Two years passed and they still remained good friends. Life was going on in its own space – but the day had finally come and it was inevitable.

It was a lazy afternoon in Meera's household, where everybody was busy taking their afternoon nap. The silence was enough to let someone believe that the house was empty, until a huge wailing sound came across from the hallway. One of the servants came running towards Vikram's mother's room. It was enough for the neighbours to believe that someone passed away. Meera ran out of her room and quizzed one of the servants.

'The war broke out across the border,' said the servant, 'the nation is in the grip of anticipation that the war would reach the city. Madam is very upset; Vikram *sahib* is going to war.'

Meera froze at the servant's reply.

The entire household was in the grip of shock, pots of chai running in and out of Meera's mother-in-law's room. Servants pranced around her with tablets for headache and blood pressure, making sure she was comfortable. 'Meera,' she said, 'you talk to Vikram and tell him not to go to war, he doesn't have to go. He is volunteering.'

Vikram interrupted Meera from making any more suggestions. 'Come on, Mother, it's not the end of the world – I will have to go. The country needs me.'

'But your mother needs you too, you are my only son. Can someone turn the TV off?'

Hearing his mother's remark, Vikram stormed out of the room in anger. Meera followed him out. 'I hope you understand, Meera, my country needs me more than anyone needs me,' he said.

'I … I do, but …'

Before Meera could say another word, Vikram took her to his arms. 'I promise you, I will be back before you know it.'

Closing her eyes, Meera wanted to feel sad – she tried, but she couldn't pretend. That was the one thing she was good at.

What would it be appropriate to do? Would it be easy to convince people she was faking her love for Vikram, or was it equally easy for Meera to hide her love for Brian?

***

It was two months and three days since Vikramaditya left for the war across the border. News channels screened the tragedies and victories of war every day. The entire nation was deep in the propaganda of a loveless calamity. There was hatred among religions; people once close were now enemies, and they were all victims.

Similarly, the household of Vikramaditya was not spared; the cook wouldn't buy milk from the usual milkman because he was from across the border. One of the butchers had to close his shop down because he spoke Urdu. His shop was burnt to ashes. People raised banners – 'You don't belong here!' – in front of mosques, ordering them to leave the country. There was no more love, only hatred and aggression.

But in between all this commotion, Meera was savouring her love for the man in her life. She hadn't stopped praying to Krishna for her love to remain in her heart forever.

There was a huge conundrum at the courtyard. There were people yelling and abusing each other. Someone must have called the police as there was a siren in the background. The guard at the gate went running towards the bungalow. '*Memsahib*! Madam! Come quickly.'

The head of the servants came running out. 'Shhh! Madam is sleeping. Could you tell the cook to behave himself and not ridicule the poor milkman? The entire neighbourhood is watching and for god's sake, who called the police?'

'It's not the police, hmm! You see.' The guard gulped, gasping for some air. He looked terrified, his face white.

'What's wrong with you? You look like as if you have seen a ghost. Or did you drink on duty again?'

'Could you just for once stop talking and come with me. It's not the police, it's the major and there's a trunk at the back with the national flag. He wants to see the Madam.'

The head servant froze at the comment of the guard. He quickly ordered everyone to empty the courtyard and asked the guard to clear everyone from there; he personally went to get Vikramaditya's mother's personal assistant.

***

The major had his head down when Vikramaditya's mother walked into the room. He took off his cap and kept his head lowered.

'No, tell me he is alive?'

'I'm sorry to say we have lost Vikram. He was a brave soldier! He and his entire battalion saved a village. They were doing their rounds of rescuing the civilians. There was a wait of two hours for the next chopper to come for the final pick-up but Vikram had a little girl from the enemy's side that was wounded from the crossfire and needed urgent medical attention. He gave up his place for her. When we came back for him, he was already hurt. He was trying to kill a sniper and he had lost a lot of blood. He died on his way to the hospital. He was brave.'

Vikram's mother was too shocked to say anything. Tears were rolling out. Then somehow she had the courage to call out one word.

'*Meera*!'

The whole household came to a standstill. Everyone came running towards the main lounge room. Her shrill voice turned into a sob, and then relentless wailing. The army major was well equipped for this; he had to take Vikram's mother into his arms and console her.

When Meera came into the room, she immediately knew what was going on. Taking her mother-in-law from the major's arm, she nodded to him. Meera was now in charge of her.

'Look, I knew this time he was not coming back. You also didn't stop him. It's your fault too. You should have pressured him to stay. It's your entire fault!'

Meera didn't say a word to her mother-in-law's absurd rudeness. She knew it was not the time to play the blame game. She just continued to console her hysterical mother-in-law, who didn't want let go of Meera.

The servants cleared the way in the courtyard for the soldiers to rest Vikram's coffin. There was already a huge crowd that gathered in the courtyard and outside the bungalow. Meera's parents were among them. Meera looked at them and smiled; she was relieved to see them.

Mrs Sen was shocked to see her daughter smiling back at them; she expected her to cry, moan, be in tears just like Vikram's mother, perhaps more of a hysterical widow. Meera was calm, composed and peaceful standing there in a white sari.

***

When the final rites were done and everyone returned to their houses from the crematorium, Meera wanted to have some time of her own. She wanted to cry but she couldn't. She wanted to laugh at her mother-in-law's hysterics and she wanted to laugh at the major; she knew if Vikram was alive he would laugh with her too, because Vikram always saw the funny side of life. She couldn't hold any longer and ran straight to her room. She closed her bedroom door and laughed until she broke into hysterical tears.

She ripped all the photos of Vikram off the wall and threw down the cupboard that was stacked with idols of Lord Krishna. The sound of the shattering glasses from the cupboard echoed through the empty hallway of her room. Meera sat among the scattered brass miniatures of Lord Krishna. She howled, lying in tears on the mess she'd created. Running her hand through the debris, she searched for the idol of Lord Krishna given to her by her uncle; unable to find it, she settled for a large brass miniature from the collection. She carefully wiped the idol with her sari to remove all the glass residue, taking it to her chest. Like a little girl, she whispered, 'I am sorry.'

'Sorry? Meera!' The entire room echoed with Lalita's laughter. Meera was too weak to respond to her. 'This is what you wanted. This is what you get when you betray a man who has been so good to you. You wanted him to die so that you can go back to Brian. Your mother-in-law knows the truth. What's the use of crying to Krishna when you couldn't sustain two men in one lifetime?' The laughter grew louder and the sarcasm grew stronger.

Meera couldn't stand her friend's disgrace anymore; she stood, clutching the idol of Lord Krishna with her right hand as she turned towards the mirror to face Lalita.

An agile but frail-framed Lalita was wrapped in a similar

white sari as Meera, her right hand also clutching the brass miniature of Lord Krishna. Her eyes were puffy with tears just like Meera's. She looked around at the vast emptiness of the room and then into the mirror. Finally, for the first time Lalita looked at Meera, and Meera was looking back at her own reflection, Lalita.

'Go away, Lalita! Go away, I don't need you anymore. I can take care of myself now; this is the path that has been chosen by Krishna for me.'

'Meera, don't be that impugned stubborn girl who couldn't do anything without me. Who will rub your tears and who will pull you together? You have no friends. You think this idol will do that for you? It is wrapped in brass. I breathe, I talk, I wipe your tears, I wrap your sari, I laugh when you laugh, I ...'

'You laugh because I laugh, Lalita. You breathe because I breathe, you wipe my tears because I wipe my tears with my hands, you wrap my sari because I wrap it with my hands. Don't you get it? You are just a figment of my imagination. I *let* you talk, damn it! *Now get out*!'

Meera took a big piece of wood from the broken cupboard and threw it across the mirror. Meera saw her image on the mirror scattering into a million pieces, but now she was only looking at herself. Lalita was now lost forever amid those broken glasses. If now she said the name of Krishna, she heard her own voice for the first time. The strong voice of Lalita was not overcoming her at all.

Meera also thought that for the first time, Krishna was smiling at her. She hugged the idol and smiled back at him.

Behind her closed door, Meera's sister-in-law was waiting with a tray of food. She heard it all.

Rebirth of Meera

It was three months and ten days since Vikramaditya's death. The entire household was still grieving, trying to come to terms with losing him. Nothing was the same. Vikramaditya's mother was still in mourning; most days she remained indoors. Her relation with Meera ended the day he died. She still continued blaming Meera for not stopping him from going to war. After her daughter narrated the whole story of Meera and Lalita, she hated her even more.

Meera confined herself to one room, totally cutting her herself from the outside world. She survived on milk and fruits. Her curtains remained closed, the only light from an oil lamp in front of Lord Krishna. The room was empty of worldly possessions: no bed, no television, no cupboard, no air-conditioning. There was only a table fan, which Meera thought of as a luxury. If she needed the air, she would open the windows of her room.

She spent her time chanting Krishna's name and totally losing herself in singing his praises. She would sing, meditate and chant so loudly that the servants thought she had gone mad after losing Vikram. Neighbours would enquire about her, and sometimes on the loud chanting that came from her bedroom.

Meera's mother-in-law got fed up with the neighbour's enquiries and also grew tired with her behaviour.

One day, on an afternoon like any other day, the entire house was quiet – but if one took notice to listen into the silence, they would hear a humming sound approaching the laneway. Meera was in her room and she could hear the distant chanting coming towards her house. She ran downstairs, into the hallway, through the garden and towards the gate. The adrenaline was too high for anyone to stop her, not even the guard.

Meera looked to her right, to her left and then straight. She closed her eyes to concentrate on the chanting. The sound grew from a hum, louder and louder, from voices to singers. There was a huge procession of people with music coming from the left, all singing and chanting in the name of Krishna. Meera's pupils dilated with the name of Krishna being chanted by many. She realised she was not alone. Her left hand clasping on her sari came loose in the shadow of the moment, released to an unstoppable thumping with the beat. From the north-east side of the street, the smell of jasmine mixed with sandalwood was enough to cloud her mind with insanity for her love of him. For Krishna.

Meera threw herself in the crowd to sing and dance; she was not in herself. She threw her hands in the air and closed her eyes, smiling and singing along with the crowd. The guard was speechless seeing her at this state. He rang into the bungalow to report what he saw.

The neighbours were out to pay alms and gifts to the devotional singers in the processions, as these were saints, holy men and devotees of Krishna collecting money for a temple. The air was thick with the smoke of incense; rose water and jasmine rained all around. In between the smoke and dust, when the haze seemed to settle a bit and the entire neighbourhood saw Meera clad in a white sari dancing with strangers, they were shocked to see her dance and sing with the commoners.

The maidservant and the guard ran out to get her but she was not in anyone's control. She was in a trance, in a higher state for her love of Krishna. She flowed with the crowd.

***

The next morning, the guard and the maidservant found Meera lying on the footsteps of their neighbourhood temple.

Meera's parents were called to take her away. Her mother-in-law advised them to get Meera checked by a good psychiatrist. She even went on to insult her, implying that she might be schizophrenic. Mr and Mrs Sen said not one word to her, instead calling for Meera.

When Meera came down in her white sari, all she wore with it was a *tulsi* (basil) necklace and bracelet. She hugged her mother and father and said to them, 'The world is one with Him – I am his now. I belong with him. Come, I will show you my love for him.'

Meera took his mother's hands and took her to her room. Mrs Sen was shocked to see her room. Her daughter now was living a life of a saint. There were no clothes to pack. No luggage for a journey. She collapsed on the floor with her hand on her forehead.

Meera, hearing her mother's sobs, took her hand. 'Don't be sad, Mother – I am now married to him. He had always been the one for me but I had failed to see it. Ever since he first came into my life with Uncle, he tried telling me something but I couldn't understand his love. Accept us, Mother. This is my new life. Bless me, for the truth has been revealed now, for what I lived until now was all a lie.'

Mrs Sen looked more concerned about her daughter's well-being; Mr Sen was concerned too but also relieved that his daughter seemed happier than ever, even when she first came to get married to Vikram.

Moving back in with her parents helped Meera to devote her life to Krishna without any restrictions. Mrs Sen called for a psychiatrist but Mr Sen stopped her. 'Let it go, we have lost her already. It's too late now. She is more happy in her world and I would rather see her happy there than in ours.'

Mrs Sen couldn't believe her husband's words. 'So you want her to become a lunatic? She already had an imaginary friend and now this absurd love for Krishna. I'd rather poison her to save her from this than let her suffer.'

'I understand your pain, Mrs Sen, but look at your daughter – she is happy. She is not mad, she knows exactly what she is doing. Maybe she is not strong as us and her weakness is her love for Krishna. Let her go.' They both hugged each other and cried.

Meera had created her own temple outside the backyard. She now wrote songs in Krishna's praises. She was now known as the recluse of the Sens. Her small room became a holy shrine, a temple; it smelled of honey, incense and the sweet perfume of the seasonal flowers. But Meera was not satisfied; she wanted to do more for Krishna.

'What more can I do to have your eternal love? Tell me,

Krishna.' She looked at the brass idol for a long time and then fell asleep at Krishna's feet. Krishna touched her hair and woke a sleeping Meera. Meera couldn't believe her eyes. 'Take my hand and just walk with me to the west. There we shall rest for eternity.' A flower fell on Meera's head, waking her from her beautiful dream.

She narrated her dream to her parents and said she had been summoned to be with Krishna in the west – but before that, she needed to marry herself to him so she could have his eternity. She was leaving for the south of the country to be a devadasi.

The next morning in her courtyard, seeing her own reflection in the little pond, her lips broke out into a little smile when a strand of hair fell in front of her face. The long locks fell one by one in front of her until she was exposed to her baldness. The once luscious black hair that was her crowning glory now rested on the grass like scattered ashes from a crematorium ground. Her pupils dilated with excitement. Rubbing her bald head, she smiled; it was a slight glimpse of her new life. *A rebirth for Krishna*, she thought.

'Thank you,' Meera said to the barber. 'I am now dressed for his service.' Devadasi – *deva* meaning god and *dasi* meaning a servant – is a girl or woman dedicated to worship and service of a deity in a temple for the rest of her life. She was now on a journey to be Krishna's wife.

She started her journey southward on foot. She was not scared anymore to face or think of what people thought about her. Their judgements and opinions did not matter. His love was her providence now. Everywhere she went, she now saw people, real people. It was now not a flower boy selling flowers anymore, but an extraordinary, young, innocent boy baking under the hot sun with sweat dripping from his forehead, his body odour overlapping with the sweet smell of jasmine and rose, trying to create a livelihood. People begged on the streets; there was a woman breastfeeding an infant, covering her shame and the baby under her sari while she kept begging for the other three children who played on the other side of the street.

A tourist bus bulging with people narrowly missed an elderly woman who couldn't walk to cross the street to go to the temple nearby; she was ignored by passers-by. Meera couldn't help herself, she ran to the woman's aid. They walked into the temple grounds and Meera sat with her outside for alms and food. Looking across the stretch of people, she felt alive from seeing the real faces of love, trying to understand how poverty and Krishna could be on their lips and on their faces, as if they have accepted this as their path of life.

She took her hands to close her ears from hearing all the voices, the laughter. She was able to listen to their whispers, the conversations with themselves they were having in their heads. Her heart raced and for a split second she thought she heard Lalita again. Her throat parched, her cheeks warm and a drop of sweat falling from her brow, she stood up too quickly and her head swung from end of the street to the other. Fatigue mixed with dizziness; she narrowly missed the corner of the footpath as the same elderly woman who was saved by Meera a while ago quickly came to her aid – now the woman was her saviour. She offered Meera her cup of water. 'Thank you!' Meera replied.

The elderly woman laughed, pointing her finger towards the temple. 'That's Krishna's miracle to send us together. *Jai shri* Krishna.'

She was struggling to understand what was going on inside her. *Does poverty drive people to kindness? Or is being rich is just a privileged word for being ungrateful?* The quest for truth was to be with Krishna, but the deeper she would go to that truth, the deeper she would be pulled by her social and moral compass. With the changes that were happening to her, one would think she was mad – but what is the definition of madness? Her frail physicality was already a living proof that society would soon label her insane, if they hadn't already. 'If your love was so easy to get, maybe it wouldn't be so hard to understand this change, the world around me. Help me.' She closed her eyes while praying, her whole life flashing in front of her like a dream. She fell asleep.

'I am here, Meera,' Vikramaditya whispered as he touched her. Her heart sank.

Looking at Meera's tears, the old lady offered her a rag covered in dirt to wipe off those tears. Meera's eyes were covered in soot; the old woman laughed at her, and Meera joined her in laughter when she saw her reflection on the puddle of water by the temple.

'Look, I have someone to show you,' said the old woman. 'He is there, a *firangi*, a white guy singing devotional songs in praises of you, Meera.' She pointed Meera to the temple.

Meera's heart sank. She ran towards the temple and saw Brian. 'No, you don't love me, Brian!' Meera screamed and Brian did not bother to look at her at all; he ignored Meera and slowly he was changing into a black man, motionless as a statue. He had a crown on his head with feathers. The temple was deserted. *How odd!* Meera thought. She could've had a life with him – that life she chose to leave behind.

'Meera! I am here! Your Krishna who's only yours,' the statue finally spoke.

She opened her eyes. She wasn't dreaming anymore; the old woman was still there, sitting beside her. Her chest wasn't tight anymore – she was calm. The people she was sitting amid were all poor, begging, eating and trying to fit within this struggle of life and living. It was not poverty that was to be blamed for her change, nor leaving behind a privileged life; neither did it have anything to do with finding Krishna amid poverty. It was a choice she made for love: her truth was Krishna and if she found Krishna, she would find love. She didn't feel sad – she felt settled. Meera was now open and aware to everything, even the slightest of whispers or tears from a stranger.

Some foreign tourists were taking photographs and happened to capture Meera's heroic save of the elderly woman. A local newspaper published a short story on the well-to-do, young, educated woman who gave up worldly things to be a devadasi. Before long, one of the country's leading newspapers wanted more detail on Meera's story.

The rest was history. The story was reprinted with more details of Meera's life on page five of a major newspaper's Sunday magazine. It read, 'The Modern Meera Bai! The story of an ordinary microbiologist and her extraordinary love for Krishna.'

Meera was soon not only catching the attention of temples and their priests, but also the media. She was now the new gossip, a topic for news. People started talking about her; stories were created, filmed and leaked into YouTube and Facebook.

Meera was once again attached to Vikramaditya's family. Her mother-in-law did not like it at all. She wanted to prove to the world that Meera was no saint; in fact, she was just a woman suffering depression after her husband's death and gone to extremes to prove that Krishna existed for her love.

The whole nation was now in Meera-mania. Newspapers, magazines, Instagram and television had Meera everywhere. Everyone followed her; there were camps in her name. Washing powder and biscuits advertisements endorsed the face of Meera; even without her endorsement, they sold like hot cakes. 'Wash your clothes with Meera washing powder and you will be eternally blessed, cost just ten rupees.' Every border she crossed to go to another state, people would wait for her with garlands. There were processions of saints and devotional singers singing *bhajans*, songs in praise of Krishna.

Meera had no idea what she had started. She innocently mixed with the crowd in celebration of Krishna's love, giving media interviews for her love of him.

After three months, she had almost completed her journey. On an evening of celebration when she was just a day from reaching her final destination, an agent hired by Vikramaditya's mother stood in the middle of a sitting crowd and asked the punters to stop the singing for now. 'I have a question for you, Meera *jee*. If you are so holy and in love with Krishna, do you think that he exists even for your death?'

The entire crowd went quiet and looked for Meera's reaction. Meera just smiled at the crowd and looked at the stranger with that odd question. She closed her eyes to pray. When she opened her eyes she smiled at him. 'Tell me how I can prove to you that there is nothing between life and death – it's all a mirage. This body is a mirage and the soul is the purest form. When I … if I die, you will cry for a body that doesn't belong to me. But what is sadness? That we will never understand. The soul is free and happy. Krishna is everything I need. Krishna will give me everything that I need from my death. Tell me then, how can I make your soul smile?'

'Meera *jee*, the soul – actually, my soul – would be happy if you could do this for me.' Taking out a glass bottle from his cloth bag, the stranger walked towards Meera to hand her that bottle.

'What is that, my friend?' someone yelled from the crowd.

'A cure for Meera *jee*'s madness?' The stranger winked at the other man.

Meera just stood there smiling. 'Come here, my dear man, give me what you bring and I shall offer to my man first before I accept your kindness. It is Him of who I sing my praises. For Him I breathe and live.'

'If that's what you breathe for and who you breathe for, then let's see if it's He who saves you from the last day for you to breathe.' The stranger lashed out those words angrily at Meera.

People were confused at the whole scene; they quite did not understand what was going on. Some men huddled around the stranger to stop him from approaching Meera. She politely told them to free the man as he didn't mean any harm; he'd brought her a gift, a 'cure' as he so proclaimed.

Everyone was up on their feet, nudging one another to see what was about to take place. They all waited in anticipation. Finally the man with his strange request went up to Meera; they were now face to face. Meera just smiled at the stranger, taking the glass bottle that had no colour – just a clear liquid floating in it. The stranger's hands trembled while giving it to Meera.

'Krishna, this is for you. I give you all my love and before I can accept this humble request, I offer you this gift of life with all my humbleness.' She closed her eyes and prayed before gulping the whole bottle.

That's suicide, it's humiliating, the stranger thought. His heart thumped. He would have no murder on his hands, just the reputation of challenging a person who thought she was a saint. No one would lose anything – except for Meera. He was also potentially committing a bigger suicide than Meera, exposing himself to fame this way.

In seconds, froth and foam were forming around Meera's mouth and she fell on the floor, spitting blood. The stranger got nervous from seeing the state of Meera. He had been assured there was no poison, just ground-up sleeping pills. *Is she playing a game too, to frame me? That's not possible!* He tried to hide his nervousness. He'd been assured that nothing would happen to her and he would become famous unmasking her, proving that she's not linked with any god.

He had to recover from this and do some quick thinking. Without wasting any more time he shouted, 'See, I told you she's nothing but a fraud. She's no god or there is no Krishna to help. Before anyone does anything to me, just be wary that I also have the antidote to save her life. There is only five minutes left to give her this antidote. So think wisely before laying your hands on me.'

People were too confused to react, but there were men gathering on the stage, huddling around the scene of the crime to catch this cold-blooded murderer and stop him from further harming Meera.

There was a lot of commotion. Someone snatched the antidote from the stranger's hand and rushed in aid of Meera. People were rushing towards Meera and towards the stranger at the same time to beat him up. Time was running out for Meera; the person who snatched the antidote from the stranger ran to Meera and forced open her mouth, quickly forcing the antidote down her throat as everyone helplessly watched her slowly die.

Then, just as they were giving up on her, she opened her eyes. She took a deep breath, wiping the foam and the blood from her mouth, and stood up with a help from an elderly woman who was wiping her forehead with her sari. The woman screamed from top of her voice. 'The antidote has worked! Meera is alive!'

'No, it couldn't work! There's no antidote, it was just water … and I didn't give her poison!' the stranger screamed. *How can that be? There was no poison or antidote, I cannot believe it,* he thought. 'It was supposed to be sleeping pills and the antidote was not meant to be anything, but just plain water. Do you understand, people? There was no poison in the first place, it was meant to be sleeping pills. I was told by the …' He stopped abruptly realising he spoke too much already. For a brief moment he felt numb, his palms sweaty and his eyes twitchy. He then knew he was framed by none other than Vikramaditya's mother for just a few thousand rupees. *Who would believe me now? It will be my word against hers*, he thought.

'It's a miracle! Miracle!' everyone screamed. 'How extraordinary! Meera is the eighth wonder of the world. A living wonder.'

'I can only die if He asks me to die. He still wants me to live and to cure us from this lie. It was a gift, my friend, so how can I die? How can I die with such sweetness of immortality? It's the ambrosia, the sweet nectar of rebirth given to me by Him.' Meera smiled at the elderly woman. 'Sing with me in praises of Krishna.' Meera thanked the person for saving her life.

The crowd cheered and they were as shocked as the stranger. People whispering to each other, 'How can this happen?' This was indeed a miracle.

The stranger kneeled down to ask for forgiveness and the crowd wanted him to be punished. 'I was just here to humiliate you, Meera *jee*, not to kill you. I was told to give you sleeping pills to make you fall asleep and then unmask you, prove that you are nothing but just an ordinary human being.' He stopped, carefully choosing his words. 'I am really sorry, I was not thinking. I am too ignorant to doubt your divinity. I swear on Krishna, I never gave you poison.' He scratched his head. All along the stranger was carrying water, lured by the prospect of being interviewed by news channels for unmasking Meera, but now he thought to have been framed. *By who?* he wondered as the police were taking him away.

'It's all okay! He just came to me to spread some love among you. So let us celebrate today for this day of creation, the creation of the truth. You fell for hatred only to fall for grace and love again. Love still prevails over everything and everyone who is temporary. So let's cherish the time today.'

Meera smiled at the crying stranger. On her orders the stranger was set free; no charges were brought against him, as she told the police, 'No one has died to be charged, and no one has committed a crime. The only crime is to mislead one's heart.'

No one knew about the biggest mystery of that day. It all fell to belief, or a myth, and that's how the headlines were created around it.

Meera's name was now forever embedded with Krishna.

***

This miracle made headlines all over the world. Newspapers usually had only space to write about war on religion or tragedies in the name of religion, but somehow they created a space in their front pages about the miracle of Meera, a little hope in the name of love amid all the hatred.

On a rainy day by the Yarra in a café, a man sipping his morning coffee read about Meera's miracle in a newspaper while in tears – a man who had forgotten to embrace her love and closed his heart forever. Brian Johnson was now crying in shame for betraying Meera.

The Truth

Zipping his pants, Brian kissed Meera on her forehead. 'I will leave you in peace now.' Brian smiled at Meera and closed the door behind him. He walked away in silence, tormented. The smell of her skin lingered upon him like a shadow of doom. Was he being a coward? Perhaps he was, but he knew that he was not so brave to embrace love. It was just not his thing.

On the contrary, Meera was falling in love with Brian. She touched her heart and looked outside her window, watching Brian walking on the empty street until he completely vanished into the darkness of the night. She stood there for a long time, thinking what it would be like if she sent him a text. Would he reply? She ran to grab her phone.

'Meera, don't do this. Listen to me, it's not love … it's just that you want this to see it as love. It's not love.'

'Lalita, have I ever asked you about your opinion? You need to feel for once what I am feeling. How can you feel my heart? How can you? When I see you in the mirror you just look back at me, trying to talk me out of things. Just go now, Lalita – I have to do this.' Meera shut Lalita out of her mind and sent a text to Brian.

'Thank you and I hope to see you again because this heart is not the same. Yours Truly, Meera.'

Brian looked at the text. He was scared. He wanted to reply but was too weak to text her that tonight was the end of them.

It was just not that one text Meera sent him; there were ten more of apologies and five more of how she missed him. There were still no replies. Brian was crumpling inside; the more he read them, the more he wanted to be with her – but the thought of being in love and being devoted to her for a lifetime scared him. He thought it over and over – what if they both turned out to be someone else, if they hated each other? And his freedom – he not only had to share his apartment, his mess, his life – he had to share hers equally too.

He was not quite prepared to do so. He had to ignore Meera. He just couldn't afford to fall in love with her. He thought that with time he would heal, not thinking that he was silently punishing a woman who was now in love with him.

Meera waited for him outside the café, near the tram stop where they first met, hoping to catch a glimpse of Brian. He would sometimes see her standing at the tram stop and he would quickly change his path. He blocked her phone number so he wouldn't see those text messages and he absorbed himself with work.

Life went on for Meera too; she totally submerged herself in work, and then one day, just as she thought she was getting over the hope of his return, her phone rang. It was Brian.

'Mee … Meera, it's me. I want to … want to see you.'

There was silence. 'Is that you, Brian?'

'Yes, it's me. I am waiting for you downstairs.'

Meera ran to get the lift to the foyer; it took the lifts forever to come. She took the stairs, running the whole six floors down. Panting for air, she screened the whole foyer searching for Brian. She couldn't see him, and ran out the sliding doors of the building. There he was, standing under a tree.

Meera couldn't move, as if she had no legs to walk. She just stood there, looking at him, still panting for air.

'Meera, how are you?' Brian looked at her and then, taking her in his arms, he ran his fingers on the side of her forehead and looked into her eyes. He hugged her. Meera was quiet, not even a smile.

'Let's go for a walk,' he said. 'It has been a long time since we last spoke. How have you been, Meera? I have been so busy caught up with work. Tell me, how have you been? Why are you so quiet?'

'It has been three years and fifty-two days since I last saw you. You tell me, how should I be?'

Meera was now crying. Brian took her into his arms and called a taxi to go to her place.

Once in her apartment, no words could be spoken anymore. She was now in tears. He lifted Meera in his arms and carried her to her bed. He kissed her and cajoled her, securing her in his arms as he rubbed her back. He kissed her, touched her face and looked into those teary eyes; he was once again in a trance. The clean smell of her skin was torturing him and then it all came back to him. They assimilated as one for the first time, making passionate love.

When Meera woke up, Brian was gone. She knew this time he loved her too. Next to her pillow, there was her notepad with fresh writing.

'If I stay, I will not be the same again. What I feel for you is important and that's how it should be remembered always. What is not important, and should be forgotten, is what I cannot give you. Yours, Brian.'

'Lalita, you were right, he is not coming back.' Meera looked at herself in the mirror, sobbing – until she heard herself in Lalita's voice ordering her to go back to her parents. 'He is not coming back,' Meera quietly said to herself in that overpowering tone of Lalita's

She looked away from the mirror to look at the idol of Krishna. 'Will you leave me too, Krishna? Is this what you have planned for me?'

She took her phone out to call her parents, who were so persistent in getting her married. All they were waiting for her to say yes. She was now ready to get married to Vikramaditya.

***

Brian looked at the photo of Meera in the newspaper: the Meera he knew was in love with him, and today the Meera the world knew was in love with Krishna. *How ironic*, he thought.

It had been three years again since he last saw Meera. She was even more beautiful than ever, even without her hair; in her white sari and sitar it seemed as though she was singing in a festival of some sort. The news piece read, 'The miracle lady is in search of love for her Krishna. Next month she travels with her followers to the west, to a festival that comes once every twelve years.' He thought to himself she had this amazing aura about her – he needed to see her again. Maybe this time he could acknowledge his love for her, win her back from the arms of Krishna and keep her to himself for the rest of his life. He had an idea!

Grabbing the newspaper under his arms, he dashed out of the café and headed straight to his office. After cutting through the bureaucratic red tape, he finally sold his story to the highest TV bidder, his fee going towards a cause for eradicating poverty in Meera's country.

Within a month, Brian collected a team of his best technicians, cameraman and sound mixer. He also hired a personal assistant who knew the country well and understood the language, especially in the west of the country where Meera would go to the holy festival. Brian put up the best show possible; for him, money was not an issue. After all, he finally understood what it felt like when someone was really gone. He was now on a mission to see her and win back her trust.

Little did he know that Meera was beyond all this – she was now somewhere between reality and in fantasy of Krishna.

***

In the following weeks, Brian and his team would reach the capital of the country. There, they would meet with representatives from a renowned local TV channel and a journalist who would not only help them with their journalist passes and clearance, but also keep them from any unstable conditions. Elections would soon be upon the country and the political scene was not stable – riots and religious war were everywhere. It was a smart move to be in their shadows.

***

The weather was too hot for them to handle but the excitement to do such an extraordinary story was like a bubble ready to burst. They travelled mostly by local trains, mingling with the locals and the followers and understanding what it meant to be one of them. For Brian, all he wanted was to feel Meera: her humility, where she belonged and what she was attached to. He wanted to understand her.

On one occasion he slept under a tree without the comfort of a pillow, drinking from the local chai stand and water pumped out of a tube-well in the middle of a field. A farmer ploughed the field close by. There was the smell of cow manure and all was there to see was this endless greenery and a tube-well in the middle of the field – all with an unknown silence that was not awkward at all. *This is providence!* he thought.

Brian's vision was obscured by the water he splashed on his face from the tube-well. He closed his eyes to envisage Meera standing in the corner. Rubbing his eyes, he felt restless; the more he thought of getting closer to Meera, the more he felt about the impossibilities. By now he had this urgent feeling of holding her in his arms to rid himself of these unsettled feelings.

He thought of making love to her again – they would make babies, creating a life for each other by the Yarra. He was lost again in his dreams for Meera. He fell on his back on the earth of the paddy green field, taking refuge under the heat of the afternoon sun melting away everything, suffocating the air – but for Brian it was just him with Meera on his mind, which was melting him to insanity.

One would think that it was all too easy for Brian as he was once a country boy, but in reality it was as hard as it looked. In a new country where everything was foreign, the only thing that kept him together were the memories of Meera, and the thought of seeing her and being with her.

***

It was sheer madness when they got to the location by the river; people were there in the thousands. There were makeshift tents, medical camps, food stands and water stations. Brian and the local journalist pitched their tents among all this commotion; they mapped the points from where they would capture the scene and who would interview whom.

The initial plan was that Brian and the local journalist would do one interview with Meera; if they got lost or a riot broke out, then they would do separate interviews. Otherwise the crew would stick together in packs. If they did get lost or if anything happened to any of the two groups inadvertently, then everyone would meet at a designated area around the other side of the river that lead to the highway around four pm local time. They would wait for an hour; if a person or group didn't return, they would head straight back to the main city, report back to the newsroom to broadcast the story and then signal for a search alert.

But Brian had his own plan.

The whole night, Brian tossed and turned; he couldn't wait to hatch his plan. It was five in the morning; everyone was fast asleep in the camp from sheer exhaustion of the heat and the day's work. From a distance there was some kind of noise. At first Brian thought people were talking, which he couldn't understand as it was in a different language, but then it became louder. He got up to walk outside and he could hear drums, music – and then singing. He rushed inside to wake up his assistant and got out his binoculars. What he saw froze him. It was Meera, and people were singing while throwing flowers in the air as if it were some sort of welcoming.

'Get up, the time has come. Pack your gear, mate. We have to reach to the vantage point,' Brian said to his assistant, nudging him. 'Remember, you ought to text the crew only if only anything happens to me, otherwise wait for a couple of hours – if I don't come back, then meet them at the stand point at four pm sharp. Don't waste time or give any inclination of my whereabouts. Under no circumstances … I repeat, *under no circumstances* you would tell them about my location. Is that understood?'

'Yes! Roger that, let's do it.' Rubbing his eyes, the assistant picked up his camera and backpack and followed his boss from behind.

***

It was almost light when they reached where Meera had camped. Brian and his assistant took refuge in a seven-storey brick house; the owner was not at all reluctant to let them in as soon as he saw 'Press' written on their cards. That meant he would be on television for sure. Brian and his assistant ran towards the terrace, the owner following behind them. The view was spectacular.

'Brian look, there she is!' said the assistant.

Brian turned back to look at the side of the crowd. He looked through his binoculars and was amazed to see what he saw. It was three long years but nothing had changed, she was still the same only now frail and now clad in a white sari.

He closed his eyes. Images of her – her smile, the dimple on her left cheek when she broke into a smile, the fragrance of her body, the touch of her lips, him playing with her long hair and caressing her cheeks, her embracing him with kisses – were all coming back to him. For a brief moment, Brian thought he was crying. He quickly dropped his camera to his side and signalled his assistant that he will join the crowd. Brian's assistant tried to stop him as it was too risky, there could be a stampede. It was a religious pilgrimage with police everywhere – anything could happen.

Every corner Brian turned, he saw the euphoric crowd dancing or throwing flowers in the air. It was getting harder and difficult for him to keep track of her. The more he tried to follow her, the more he would be sucked in by the crowd and pushed into the opposite direction. The air around him was hot and stuffy. It was suffocating.

Then he was pushed towards a small group within the crowd. The pushing and shoving formed a gigantic chain of humans falling on top of each other in a domino effect. Dust and sand filled the air from the riverbanks.

Time froze for Brian; he narrowly escaped the stampede. He wouldn't have been that lucky if someone from that crowd hadn't pulled him towards the corner of the scaffolding.

Brian rubbed the dust out of his eyes to see who this Good Samaritan was, expecting he would still be there. He looked in awe. It felt hard to breathe, as if he were in a trance –some sort of a mystical dream, or an out of body experience.

She smiled at him; Brian remembered that same smile when he first met her.

The only thing he could say was 'Meera! Meera, it's me, Brian! I am here … do you recognise me?'

'Take my hand, Brian … come with me.' Meera smiled at Brian.

They walked by the river towards a temple, away from the crowd on an unpaved empty dirt road. For the first time since he had come here, Brian could now hear the sound of the river flowing beside them. Suddenly he had a sense of calmness around and about him. The word 'peace' was a language he never understood and today it was translating itself to him, just by being with Meera.

Brian stopped and kneeled in front of her. 'I am tired, Meera … I am tired of running away from you. I cannot do this anymore. I lied. The truth is I loved you since the first day I saw you. I need you for us – not for me, for us. I am incomplete without you, can't you see? I am scared, Meera. I am scared.' Brian was now gulping through his tears, weeping like a little boy who'd lost his way back home.

Meera cupped his chin in her hands and looked at his helplessness. 'There is nothing to be scared of, my beloved – I was always with you then, and now … I will always be with you. However, what you want is a mirage of me,' Meera said, smiling at Brian. 'Go back to your world. Go back!' she whispered.

Slowly her hands slipped away from Brian's face as she walked towards the temple. Brian remained inconsolable; he looked at her slowly vanishing along the dirt road. He gathered himself and ran after her, towards the temple; it took him a good ten minutes to find her again.

'Meera! Meera! Meera!' Brian screamed.

Meera turned to look at Brian for one last time and faced the temple doors as they opened from inside. No one was there – not a soul in sight for anyone to open those doors. *How can that be?* he thought.

Brian saw Meera walking inside the temple, the doors shutting behind her.

Brian ran towards the temple door; with great force he tried to open them, then he banged on the doors screaming Meera's name, but there was no response. In a rage, he ran around the temple to see if there were any windows, but the temple had only one door.

Fatigue and emotion were overcoming Brian; he sat down on the foot of the temple weeping as a defeated man, losing his love to another man.

All he could hear was his own weeping, birds chirping in a distance and the silent hum of the river that flowed beside him. He turned to look at the river; closing his eyes, he moaned in his own grief. Images of Meera flashed through his eyes. Her disappearance inside the temple, her in the crowd, her on the tram in the city of Yarra, her alone in the café – everything seemed to go from present to past for him. He fell into a deep sleep.

Brian rubbed his nose; he frowned at the smell of jasmine and incense coming from the temple. He opened his eyes and rubbed his nose at the smell. By the time he got up, his eyes still swollen with tears, the sun was fading behind the temple. The temple door was now open and he could see a piece of Meera's sari on the temple floor. He ran inside.

What he saw was beyond his understanding. The idol of Krishna was wrapped in Meera's sari. *How is that even possible?* There was a bright light beaming on the background, almost blinding Brian's eyes. He covered his face with both hands.

'Come with me, Brian – love is the only truth.'

'Meera, is that you?' Brian screamed.

'Yes! Come, give me your hand, this is providence. You, me and Krishna.'

'I cannot see you, Meera.'

'Just give me your hand, Brian; just reach out for my hand. I am here.'

Following the trail of her voice, Brian reached out for Meera's hands. The touch of her hand was electrifying; he jolted and opened his eyes. The sensation was so real that it made him sit right up. He was drenched in sweat, the sun was slowly fading away and the hum of the river was now the only thing he heard. Brian pinched himself this time to see if this was reality. He frowned, 'So it is,' he said to himself.

Brian smiled as a teardrop fell on his left cheek. Taking off his shirt, he walked into the river, which submerged him in its strong flowing current. He closed his eyes and dipped his head into the water, never to rise again.

Epilogue

When people came searching for Meera in the temple, the doors of the temple were open. They found her white sari lay across wrapped on the idol of Krishna.

Many believed to have seen her in the pilgrimage; some spotted her in the country's east.

No one knows what happened to Meera. She was forever written as the other lover of Lord Krishna, or the stone lover: this was the complete love story of Krishna and her incomplete love with Brian.

Some days later, Brian's body washed up on banks on the other side of the river. No one knew why Brian came to that village besides doing a story on a saint. He forever had an incomplete love from Meera – but in many ways, he completed his love with Meera.

'Why love still prevails around hatred.
Why hatred is so easily witnessed.
Why do we justify it with blame?'

'Abandon "fear",
it doesn't need to be brave
just do something with a smile to others
and to yourself.
Have a say, have your say.'

'If world holds you as a victim
pay a ransom to yourself
to break free from it.'

'If one friend has left you for another
why worry when there is a whole world waiting for
you
to be your family?'

'If they kiss you to sleep with you
let them taste your innocence
and then let go of them
in exchange of nothing.
Why take sex so seriously for love
when you were a transaction to them
to be completed?
Play their game and clear the clutter
for love doesn't walk under their shadows.'

'If you have one dollar in your pocket,
expect there is more to come
from where it came from.'

'Why be sad when a father has lost his memory of the present?
Why not cherish the moment of him being here
in the present
giving yourself an opportunity to reflect on him
with him in your past?'

'Why be disappointed
if a sister cannot be open with her emotions with the other?
Just embrace time
and leave the communication open
for another day to discover
This is life, so why be fragile,
when you can be so agile
taking every risk and flow through the deformity of life
so you can be reborn in this circle again.'

Nandita

Mirabai

Mirabai (1498–1547 AD), also known as Meera Bai, was born in Rajasthan; she is believed to be the most pious and spiritual Hindu mystical singer and devotee of Lord Krishna. Her *bhajans*, or prayerful songs to Lord Krishna, are still sung today as *kirtans*, meaning 'singing' in Sanskrit. She was a powerful figure and one of the most expressive and suggestive *sant*, or holy person, of the Bhakti movement in India.

The Bhakti movement formed out of the rise of folk songs, chanting of praises, and beliefs in Lord Krishna in what is popularly known the 'Age of Vaishnavi'.

Meera was born as a Rajput princess. Her unending love for Lord Krishna from the age of five was recorded in history. There is a myth about her love for Lord Krishna; it is believed that she'd once seen a wedding procession and asked her mother where her bridegroom was. On hearing this, her mother took her in front of the family idol of Lord Krishna.

The other ancient myth was that Meera's father was a devotee to Lord Krishna, and it was he who had planted the first seed of love in Meera's heart. One day, when a saint visited the house of Meera, he had with him an idol of Lord Krishna. Meera was instantly infatuated with the idol. When the idol was taken away from her, she was in an incorrigible state, filled with tears and anger. The saint tried telling her that she would not be able to look after the idol and keep it happy, and Lord Krishna was taken away from her.

She had to possess that idol at any cost, such was her love and devotion. Along with a friend and her cousin, she went to the saint's house. They were startled to see that whatever the saint offered to the idol of Lord Krishna, the deity would refuse. Suddenly, the idol started crying. On seeing this remarkable miracle, the saint was shocked. He had no choice but to return the idol to her, and that idol remained with her forever.

That day went down in history as the day Meera had found her beloved, her husband. She was only five years old when she created this unique bond between herself and Lord Krishna, and she was forever known in Hindu mythology as 'The Other Lover Of Krishna' or 'The Stone Lover'.

She was married in her early twenties, but was unhappy with her marriage. The only husband that she had sought was Lord Krishna. How could she overlook the most benevolent? She was Krishna's wife forever. She was married to a Rajput; it was an arranged marriage to the Rajputana Gharana.

The Mughal Empire soon cast its eyes on Hindustan, which is now India. Those who supported the sultanate survived the barbaric atrocities of the regime, and those who did not had to fight for freedom. It is believed that her husband was killed in this battle.

After the loss of her husband, she didn't want to believe in anything that was temporary, and her dismay turned to eternal love – which cannot be lost forever, but only felt.

It is believed that during this time, several attempts were made on her life. She was almost poisoned by her own family. At first, her love of the Lord Krishna was concealed as a private family matter, but soon Meera was running around the streets and singing songs of love for Lord Krishna, speaking to the commoners and praising his devotions. Her songs were filled with passion and longing for her Lord Krishna. She sought a place in his eternal love and his spiritual acceptance. She was a recluse. She was neither shameful nor careful in her philandering. She was defamed, she was hot gossip, and she was judged by every eye that looked upon her.

Once, she was tricked into drinking poison because someone made her believe that it was *prasad* of Lord Krishna. Such was Lord Krishna's love for Meera that he turned the poison into *amrit* (nectar).

About the Author

Nandita Chakraborty was born in Kolkatta, India, in 1975, in a small conservative family associated with the arts. Her father won many accolades in the field of Indian Cinema, so the house was always filled with creativity.

After studying, Fashion and Visual Merchandising, Nandita forged a successful career, but eventually grew to feel personally and creatively unfulfilled.

She began to write

At first, it was poetry, and then short stories that she didn't consider very good, and which she binned, but she persevered until she was writing for Melbourne newspapers and magazines. It was a steep learning curve, and in 2013 self-published her first novel, *Missing Peace*.

She took time off and travelled through India for six months, where she began to understand the pandemonium of Krishna's devotees.

One night, by chance, she caught a classic Indian movie about Mirabai – a movie she'd seen as a child, but never understood. Now it opened up to her and inspired her, and she undertook extensive research, learning that Mira Bai was a devotee of Krishna and a mystic Hindu poet.

Following three years of further research, Nandita learned there was a story to be told, a legacy of love, divinity, and sacrifice, that needed to be shared with generations to come.

Hence, *Meera Rising* was born.

Nandita wants to advocate that love and miracles do happen. She feels that Mirabai could be living amongst us, and can be that unassuming neighbour, that friend or that mysterious person who would come of age to be a great advocate of love and peace.

Her forthcoming books will always have characters that define this love, and her central protagonists will be women.

Her upcoming book, *Rosemary's Retribution*, is also about women defining themselves in love and all that empowers in its name.

www.ingramcontent.com/pod-product-compliance
Lightning Source LLC
Chambersburg PA
CBHW030532310726
48979CB00010B/1889/J

* 9 7 8 1 9 2 5 5 8 5 6 9 8 *